KU-156-769

Peter Grant

SHADOW THE SHEEP-DOG

SHADOW THE SHEEP-DOG

by

Enid Blyton

COLLINS
LONDON AND GLASGOW

First printed in this edition, 1950

PRINTED AND MADE IN GREAT BRITAIN BY
WM. COLLINS SONS AND CO. LTD.
LONDON AND GLASGOW

CONTENTS

CHAPTER ONE

THE THREE PUPPIES

ONCE UPON A TIME three small fat puppies lay in a barrel lined with warm straw. They were brown and white and almost as round as the barrel.

"You are the best puppies in the world!" their mother said to them each day as she licked them with her soft pink tongue. They pushed against her and made little puppy noises.

A big farmer came to the barrel and looked inside it. "Well, Jessie!" he said to the mother-dog. "And how are those fat puppies of yours?"

Jessie looked up at her master with her great brown eyes and waved her feathery tail. She was a beautiful sheep-dog, a clever collie who knew every inch of the hills around. For a little while she was having a rest from her work, and was looking after her family of puppies. They were nearly three weeks old, and all of them could see now. They had been born with their eyes shut, but one by one their blue puppy-eyes had opened, and now they watched the world outside the barrel, and wondered about it.

"Well, Jessie, you've three fine pups," said her master. "Hie, Johnny, have you seen the puppies to-day?"

A small boy ran up and grinned down at Jessie. "Of course I have!" he said. "I've seen them about a hundred times, haven't I, Jess?"

The sheep-dog wagged her tail, and one of the puppies tried to bite it. The boy laughed.

"Dad, let's keep one of the pups," he said. "I'd

so much like a dog of my own. I'd like that one with the white mark on its forehead."

"No—we've got enough dogs," said his father. "Give Jessie some fresh water, Johnny—she's spilt it all."

He went off, and Johnny ran to get some water. He brought back the dish and set it down. He patted Jessie on her soft head.

"That little pup is just exactly like you, Jess," he said. "I'd so much like him. Wouldn't you like to keep just *one* of your pups?"

Jessie wagged her tail. She couldn't imagine anyone being so cruel as to take her puppies away from her. She did not know that puppies and kittens go to new homes as soon as they are old enough.

The three puppies grew and grew. Jessie was a good mother, and took care of them well. The one like her was a merry fellow. He played with her tail, bit her nose, worried her ears, and tried to frighten her with his funny puppy-barks.

Soon they were all old enough to scamper about the yard. Johnny had fun with them then! Every time they saw him they ran at his ankles, got between his legs and nearly upset him.

"Johnny always looks as if he he is going in for an obstacle race when he goes across the yard with the puppies!" laughed his mother. "They're a fine family. But it's time they went to their new homes now."

Johnny was sad. Jessie was unhappy. They were *her* puppies. Why should they be given away? Did people give away their children to other families? No, they didn't. Well then, why should anyone give away Jessie's puppies?

But it was no use. Homes were found for the three puppies, and their new owners promised to fetch the pups the next week. Johnny's mother said she would be glad when they were gone now, because they had each found their way to the kitchen, and were under her feet all day long.

"That little pup like Jessie is the worst of the lot!" she said. "His nose is in everything! He'd better go first."

"Oh, *no*, Mother! I love him the best!" said Johnny. "He must be the last."

Jessie knew that her pups were going away. She spoke to them sadly. "Soon you will leave this first home of yours," she said. "You will go out into the world, and have a new master and mistress. You must be brave and good dogs, always do what you are told, and never use your teeth on anyone unless your master orders you to."

"Are you coming with us?" asked the puppies, half frightened.

"Of course not," said the big sheep-dog. "I have my work to do here. Look—here comes someone to take one of you. I wonder which it will be."

A farmer came up with Johnny's father. They stood and looked into the barrel. The puppies all ran out and scampered around the legs of the two men. One pup tried to bite at the leather gaiters of the visitor.

"He's a fine fellow!" said the farmer, picking up the puppy in a big hairy hand. "He'll do for me! I'll take him off now. Say good-bye to your mother, little fellow."

Jessie gave her puppy one last lick. She sniffed at the farmer's boots. "Good-bye," she said to her pup, who was feeling very excited and grown-up all of a sudden. "This man is a good one, but bad-tempered. See that you do all you are told or you will be well whipped."

The puppy trotted off on his short legs after his

new master. His tail wagged. He felt so grand that he could hardly bark good-bye to his two brothers.

They stood and watched him. One puppy wanted to go with him, but the other pup was glad not to leave his mother. Johnny came up and saw that one puppy was missing.

"Bother! One gone already," he said. "That's the worst of puppies and kittens—they go off to new homes as soon as they are big enough to play with!"

Next day somebody came for the second puppy. It was Mrs. Hillocks, who lived down in the village. Jessie was glad to see her, for Mrs. Hillocks was a kind old woman. She kept a poultry-run at the back of her house, and wanted a dog to guard it for her. She looked at the two puppies. One crouched down beside Jessie, afraid of leaving her, but the other trotted up and pawed her ankles.

"You're the one for me!" said the old lady. "You won't let any foxes or tramps get my hens, will you? You're a grand little dog, you are! Come away with me."

That was the second puppy. For two or three days nobody came for the third one. He missed his brothers terribly. He whined for them and hunted for them all over the place. Johnny was sad for him, and whistled to him whenever he came near.

The puppy soon followed Johnny everywhere. He trotted along at Johnny's heels, and the boy laughed at the little fat creature.

"You're like my shadow, following me wherever I go!" he said. "I wish you were mine. I'd call you Shadow!"

"Johnny, Johnny! That puppy has got to be sent away by rail," shouted his father. "Get a box and put some straw in it, and a big biscuit. Give him a drink before he goes. Put him on the farm-cart and I'll take him down to the station."

Johnny was cross. He hated the last puppy to go. But he had to obey his father, so very soon the puppy was safely in the box, with straw around him and a big biscuit to gnaw. He whined and tried to get out. Jessie ran to the box and spoke to him.

"It's your turn now. Be good and brave and obedient, and remember that you are a fine sheep-dog. Good-bye, little puppy!"

The box jolted on the farm-cart all the way to

the station. It was rather near the edge—and suddenly an extra big jolt shook the box right off the cart on to the road. The farmer was just shouting at his horse at that moment, and he noticed nothing.

The bump shook all the breath out of the puppy's body—and then he saw that the side of the box had been broken by the fall. In a trice he was out of the box and tearing home on his short puppy-legs for all he was worth. He had escaped.

"Woof, woof!" he cried to his mother, when he scampered into the yard. "I'm back! Woof, Johnny, I'm back!"

"Gracious! How did you get out of the box, you rascal?" said Johnny, hugging the puppy. "Well, well—you'll have to go by to-morrow's train."

The farmer was most astonished to find box and puppy gone when he reached the station—but he found the box on the way home, so he guessed what had happened. The puppy was put into another box the next day, and this time he arrived safely at the station. The guard put him on the train in the box, and with a loud whistle the train left the station.

The puppy was terrified. He hated the rumble

of the train. He hated the whistle. He shivered and trembled and whined. The guard took no notice. The train stopped at the next station, and the guard left his van to go on to the platform. The puppy lifted up his voice and whined piteously.

A little girl heard him. She peeped into the guard's van. "What *can* be the matter with the animal in that box?" she thought. "Is it hurt? I'll look and see."

She lifted up the lid—and in two shakes of a duck's tail the puppy leapt out, jumped down on to the platform, rushed out of the gate and tore up the dusty country lane! He didn't know where he was. He didn't know where he was going—but he was happy because he had got out of that dreadful box and away from that roaring train!

After a bit he stopped and lifted his nose into the air. He sniffed. Which was the right way home? He stood for a moment and then into his head came the way to go. He must turn the corner and go across those fields. He didn't know why he must go that way. He only knew it was the right way home.

And after about half an hour a very tired, thirsty, foot-sore puppy limped in at the farm-yard gate. How good it was to be back! There were the hens. There was the duck-pond—and there was dear old Johnny! With a whine the puppy ran limping over the yard—and Johnny stared at him in the utmost astonishment.

"What! You back *again!* However did you escape this time? I never in my life knew a puppy so determined as you! Dad! Dad! Here's the last pup back again."

The farmer came out of his shed and stared in surprise. "We can't seem to get rid of him!" he said. "He's a bold little fellow."

"Dad! Can't I keep him!" cried Johnny, picking up the trembling puppy. "I do love him so, and he's such friends with me. He'll always come back, no matter how often we send him away. I'm sure he will."

"Well—it's quite certain he wants to stay here," said the farmer. "All right—you can keep him. I like him myself—he's a good little chap. He can be yours—but see you train him well with the sheep, for he's got to earn his keep like the other dogs, Johnny!"

"Oh, Dad! Thanks!" cried Johnny, and he tore indoors to tell his mother. He put down the puppy, who at once ran at his heels as he always did.

"Mother! The pup's back again—and I'm to keep him for my own!" cried Johnny. "Do you know what I'm going to call him? I shall call him Shadow—for he follows me about just like my shadow does. Oh, I'm so happy with a dog of my own. Shadow! Shadow! How do you like your name?"

"Woof!" said Shadow, and wagged his tail proudly. He had a name. He had a master. He had a home. He was a proper dog now—and tails and whiskers, he'd show everyone he was worth keeping!

CHAPTER TWO

SHADOW LEARNS SOME LESSONS

JOHNNY WAS so pleased to have a dog of his own that he couldn't bear to part with him, even at night. He smuggled him up the stairs and into his bedroom, and very soon Shadow was sleeping at the foot of the boy's bed, on a bit of old blanket.

Johnny didn't tell his mother about this. He

knew he should have asked her, but he was afraid she would say no. All the same it wasn't very long before Mother found out—she was so surprised to find a bit of old blanket on Johnny's bed each morning.

"Johnny," she said, holding out the blanket to him, "this smells of puppy-dog. Is Shadow sleeping at the foot of your bed?"

"Yes, Mother," said Johnny. "I do love him so. He keeps my feet warm—and oh, Mother, he makes the funniest puppy-noises in his sleep. Don't say he must go and sleep out in the yard."

Mother laughed. "What a funny lot boys are!" she said. "I wouldn't have a dog in my bedroom for anything—but your father is always worrying me to let him have Jessie. And my two brothers, your uncles, had three dogs in their rooms at night! Well—I suppose if you want it so much, you must have your way. But I warn you, if I find any smelly old bones in your bed I'll shoo Shadow out every night myself, Johnny!"

"Oh, Mother, thank you!" cried Johnny, delighted, and he gave his mother a hug. "I'll see that Shadow doesn't dirty my bedroom at all. He's a really good dog. I do love him when he nibbles my toes in the morning, Mother, to wake me up!"

So all night long Shadow slept at Johnny's feet, and all day long he ran at Johnny's heels. Johnny was his master. Johnny was the most marvellous person in the world to Shadow. Nothing that Johnny could do was wrong, and if the boy was sad or somebody scolded him, Shadow's tail would go right between his legs, and he would whine as if he had been scolded himself.

"Shadow, you must learn some lessons now," said Johnny to his puppy one day. "Jessie, your mother, has taught you quite a lot of things, but I must teach you some too. You must learn to know my whistle and come at once when you are called, no matter WHAT you are doing. That's the first lesson. I'll teach you to-day."

Shadow listened, his tail wagging like a windmill. What an easy lesson! He already knew Johnny's whistle by heart. He knew his shout too. There was no voice in the world like Johnny's, Shadow was sure. He loved Johnny's smell too. Even Johnny's footsteps smelt of Johnny. Sometimes Shadow would find some in the yard and would spend a lovely minute following up the smell of the footprints until he came to Johnny himself.

"You have a sharp nose, Shadow," Johnny said to him. "That's good. One day it may be useful to you, if a sheep is lost."

Johnny took Shadow out into the fields. Shadow loved the fields because of the exciting smells everywhere. He ran about, his nose to the ground, smelling rat, mouse, hedgehog, rabbit, hare, and fox. Oh, delicious! Too exciting for words, Shadow thought. He put his head down a rabbit-hole and a big smell of furry rabbit came up.

Shadow went quite mad. He began to sniff and scrape, his nose well down the hole. Johnny smiled a little and went on down the field, leaving Shadow behind. Now the puppy was to get his first lesson!

When he was at the end of the field, Johnny stopped. Shadow was still scraping at the rabbit-hole. Johnny whistled. "Pheeeeeeeeeeee!"

Shadow heard the whistle—but how could he leave this exciting rabbit-smell? Why, he might get to the rabbit in half a minute! He took no notice of Johnny's whistle and went on sniffing and scrabbling.

"PHHHHHHHEEEEEEEEEEE!" The whistle came again, much louder. Shadow took his head out of the hole. He saw Johnny waiting for him. He wondered if he should go. No—Johnny could wait a minute till he got that rabbit! And into the hole went his eager puppy-head again.

Then Johnny shouted loudly: "Shadow! Shadow! Come here!"

But still Shadow didn't come. He felt that he couldn't leave such a wonderful rabbit-smell. And then Johnny walked all the way back till he came to the puppy. Shadow felt a sharp hand smack him, and he yelped. He took his head out of the hole and looked up in astonishment at Johnny. Johnny had smacked him! Oh, what a very dreadful thing!

"Shadow! You heard me whistle, Pheeee, and you didn't come. You heard me call you loudly, and you didn't come. You are a bad dog."

Poor Shadow! His tail was lost between his legs, his ears drooped, he couldn't look at Johnny. He crept after him, whining softly, the most unhappy and ashamed dog in all the world. Never, never would he put a rabbit-hole before his master again.

When they came to another rabbit-hole Johnny stopped. "Rabbits!" he said. "Rabbits! Go in and fetch them then."

Shadow at once went to scrape and sniff at the hole, and in a trice Johnny ran down the field. He turned and whistled. He must see if the puppy had learnt his first lesson! "PHEEEEEEEE!" The whistle went loud and clear over the field.

And this time Shadow took his head out of the hole at once, and tore off to Johnny as fast as his legs could carry him! He wasn't going to be punished again!

"Good dog, Shadow, good dog!" said Johnny, and he patted the puppy proudly. "It didn't take you long to learn that lesson, did it! I don't believe you'll need teaching that one again."

He certainly didn't. At the first sound of Johnny's shrill whistle, Shadow always bounded off to him at once. Then he was taught his next lesson—to walk exactly at Johnny's heels when he went into the town, or for walks.

"You see, Shadow, a good-mannered dog must walk just behind his master, so as not to get in his way," said Johnny. "And he must always be at heel in case he is wanted. So when I say, 'Heel!'

to you, you must walk just there—that's it—your nose almost touching my shoe. When I say 'Run, Shadow,' you may leave my heels and go bounding about for a run."

Shadow listened hard. He didn't much like walking just behind Johnny in the town. There were so many things to see and smell there. He wanted to stop and sniff at everything. He wanted to run up to the dogs he met and tell them about Johnny.

But Johnny carried a little twig, and every time Shadow's nose came too far in front instead of keeping to heel, the little twig stung the puppy's nose. So he soon learnt that Johnny meant what he said. "Heel" meant walking behind, and nothing else—he mustn't loiter, and he mustn't push in front. He was a clever little dog, so it didn't take him more than two days to learn *that* lesson.

Johnny never really hurt Shadow, but his father had told him that, like children, a dog has to be trained, and if he disobeys he must be punished. So the boy was strict with his puppy, because he loved him and wanted him to grow up into a well-trained and good dog.

"Now you must teach him to be 'On guard,' Johnny," said his father. "That is important for a sheep-dog."

So Shadow was taught what "On guard" meant. It was not so easy to learn that! Johnny took him into a field and put his cap down on the grass, and his coat. He made Shadow sit on them.

"On guard!" he said. "On guard, Shadow! You mustn't leave my hat and coat till I come back or whistle to you. You are guarding them."

"Woof," said Shadow happily. He liked sitting on anything belonging to Johnny. Johnny began to walk away. At once Shadow bounded after him, leaving the hat and coat. Johnny swung round and looked down at him sternly.

"Didn't I tell you to guard them!" he cried. "Bad dog! Go back. On guard, I tell you, on guard."

He took Shadow back to his hat and coat and made him sit on them again. Shadow's tail drooped. He didn't want to stay with a hat and coat. He wanted to go with Johnny.

Johnny set off again. Shadow waited till he had turned a corner and then bounded after him. But no, that was not the right thing to do at all!

Johnny spoke angrily to him, and Shadow was miserable. Perhaps the hat and coat were very important, he thought.

"Have I got to take you all the way back again!" cried Johnny. "Bad dog. I put you on guard, on guard, on guard!"

Shadow understood. He had to go back and stay with that silly coat and cap till further orders. Well—he didn't understand *why*—but all the same he knew he must obey. So back he went of his own accord, and lay down on the coat, his chin on his two front paws. Anyway, it was nice to smell Johnny's smell coming from the coat.

Johnny went into the next field and waited a few minutes. He peeped through the hedge and saw that Shadow was really on guard this time. "What a good little fellow he is!" thought the boy proudly. "Now I'll go back and give him a biscuit for a reward. It was hard for him to learn that lesson."

He went back. Shadow saw him coming and stood up joyfully, his tail wagging wildly. But he didn't leave the coat. No—he knew that he was meant to stay with it, on guard until Johnny came right up to him.

And then it was worth being taught the lesson when Johnny fed him with a delicious biscuit and patted him and told him he was the most marvellous dog in the world! Shadow rolled over on his back, put all his fat legs into the air and yelped for joy.

Johnny put on his coat and cap. "Another lesson learnt!" he said. "Good dog!"

Shadow learnt to let Johnny take away his bone from him, without growling or snapping. He learnt to track Johnny wherever he was, even when he was a mile or two away. That was really clever. Johnny would shut him up in a kennel, and go off by himself. Then, half an hour later a farm-hand would let him out and say, "Now find Johnny! Go find Johnny, Shadow! Where's Johnny!"

And Shadow would put his nose to the ground and run wildly about until he found a fresh footstep of Johnny's. Then off he would go, like an arrow from a bow, smelling Johnny's track without a mistake. Over field and hedge, ditch and stream, he would run—and at last would find Johnny, hidden up a tree, or in the heather!

"Good dog! You've only taken ten minutes this

time!" cried Johnny. "Do you like your lessons, Shadow? You learn them quickly enough! Soon you must go off with the other sheep-dogs and learn how to round up the sheep. I guess you'll be the cleverest sheep-dog Daddy's ever had on the farm. You will try hard, won't you, Shadow?"

"Woof," said Shadow, licking his master's hand over and over again. He was excited to hear he was to go with the big dogs. Ah—he would show them how clever he would be with the sheep!

CHAPTER THREE

SHADOW AND THE OTHER DOGS

ON THE FARM were many dogs. There was Jessie, Shadow's mother, who guarded the house and yard. Then there were Tinker, Rafe, Dandy, and Bob, all sheep-dogs except Bob, who was a mongrel. He was a queer-looking dog, with a big head, long body, feathery tail, and strong, swift-running legs. He was black and brown and had a curly coat.

Shadow was afraid of Bob. Bob was not playful, and growled if Shadow came near. He belonged to Andy the shepherd, and lived with him in his little hut on the hillside. The other dogs lived on the farm itself, but often went with Andy to round up the sheep.

Tinker was a friendly dog, whose tail was always wagging, and who was ready to push his nose into anybody's hand. Shadow loved him and ran with him whenever he could.

"You're growing!" said Tinker to Shadow. "Time you learnt something, young pup!"

"I've learnt a lot!" said Shadow. "I'm a clever dog. Johnny says so."

Tinker sprang at Shadow in play and rolled him over. Shadow tried to get away, but Tinker held him by the neck and he couldn't.

"Not so clever as you thought you were!" said Tinker. "If a dog springs on you, you shouldn't turn over on your back like that, young pup. Stand firm!"

Rafe and Dandy came up, their tails wagging. They were all good friends. Rafe was a wonderful sheep-dog, and had won many prizes for his cleverness in rounding up sheep in the hillside. Dandy was clever, too, but had a bad habit of going off by himself at times, which made the farmer angry.

The three dogs had a rough-and-tumble fight, pretending to snap and growl at one another, each trying to get hold of the other's throat. Shadow watched them.

"Let me join in," he said, and in the pup went, putting his small strength against the grown dogs. They were kind to him and let him worry them and snap at their ears.

"You'll be a strong dog one day!" said Dandy, shaking Shadow off, and pushing him right over. "We'll teach you a few things each day now. Come along and see us round up the sheep to-morrow."

"But be careful of Bob," said Tinker. "He won't stand any nonsense from you, young pup. If he tells you to do anything, you do it!"

Shadow ran joyfully to Johnny, his tail wagging hard. "Wuff!" he barked. "I'm to go and join the big dogs to-morrow. What do you think of that, Johnny?"

"I think you're just the most marvellous puppy in the world!" said Johnny, patting the fat little puppy on the head.

The next day Shadow ran off to the shepherd's hut with Tinker, Rafe, and Dandy. Bones and biscuits, how grand he felt to be out with the big dogs! He found it difficult to run as fast as they did, but he did his best.

"Now listen to me," said Tinker. "The sheep are on these two hills to-day, but the shepherd wants them to go to the next hill. We've got to take them there."

"What do we do then?" asked Shadow. "Just go in front and lead them?"

"Listen to him!" said Bob, who was near by, looking rather bad-tempered, for he always thought that he could manage to do all the work alone, and he didn't like the other dogs coming along to join him. "Silly little pup! You try leading the sheep, puppy! Run along and wuff to them and tell them all to follow you!"

"All right, Bob," said Shadow, who felt sure he could manage anything. He had always been told that sheep were very stupid, but surely they knew enough to follow a dog who was to take them to a new hillside.

So off went Shadow, wagging his tail. Bob sat down to watch, his pink tongue hanging out. The other three ran around, sniffing, but all of them watched Shadow too. They knew quite well what was going to happen.

Shadow ran up to the nearest bunch of sheep and barked to them. "Wuff, wuff! Follow me! I will take you to a fine new hillside where the grass is green and sweet."

As soon as Shadow came near the bunch of sheep, they all ran away. How very annoying!

Shadow ran after them. "Wuff! Don't be frightened of *me*, sillies! Stay and listen."

The sheep ran away again, and soon all the flock was galloping about in fright. Then the shepherd came out of his hut and shouted sternly to Shadow.

"Now then, you! What do you think you are doing? Leave the sheep alone. Chasing sheep like that—and you a sheep-dog too. You'll be no use if you start that game! Bob—put the sheep in that corner, and keep them quiet until I'm ready to move them."

Bob shot off like an arrow from a bow. He first went to Shadow and snapped at him, making that surprised little puppy rush off in fright, his tail between his legs. He ran to Tinker.

"Why is the shepherd cross? Why did Bob snap at me? Didn't I do right?"

"Watch Bob," said Rafe. All four dogs watched Bob. Bob ran all round the flock, making darts at any sheep that tried to get away. Soon he had them in a big bunch, and then running to and fro, he got them into a corner of the big hillside field. Then he lay down in front of them, watching, with one eye on his master, and one ear cocked to hear any further orders.

"Good dog, Bob," shouted the shepherd. Bob cocked the other ear and wagged his tail a little.

"Did you see how Bob did that?" said Dandy. "You've got to *make* sheep do things, Shadow, not ask them! They are such stupid creatures that they can only run away—and your job is to make them run in the right direction, without frightening them too much."

"Bob is very clever," said Shadow. "Now what are we going to do? Are we going to take the sheep across to the other hill?"

The shepherd shouted to the dogs. "Hie, Rafe, Tinker, Dandy—go and help Bob. Take the sheep down the hill, across the bridge over the stream, through the gap in the hedge and on to the hill over there."

He pointed with his stick as he spoke. The dogs went off at once, eager to be at work. Bob leapt to his feet and looked round at the other dogs. Shadow could quite well see that *he* was head of them all.

"Woof," said Bob, and every dog knew what he meant. Rafe was to go behind the sheep. Tinker was to be on guard near the bridge to make sure that the sheep went over. Dandy was to run round them with Bob, and make them go the right way.

The shepherd went into his hut, and left the dogs to do their work. He knew that he could trust them.

Shadow went with Dandy. "Now keep up with me and do as I do," panted Dandy. "It's our job to keep the sheep in a bunch and to make them run out of this field, down the hill to the stream. Bob is taking that side of the flock—we'll take this side. As soon as you see a sheep getting loose from the flock, run at it, and head it back."

My goodness, what an exciting time Shadow had! The sheep were silly, and two or three would keep getting away from the flock. Shadow tore after them, ran round to the front of them and headed them back. He was so excited that he barked loudly.

"Stop that!" ordered Bob. "We only bark when we must. If you *really* frighten the sheep they will all run away and we'll have a dreadful job getting them back. If you can't hold your tongue, go back to the farm."

Shadow was ashamed. He didn't want to go back to the farm, with the hens, pigs and ducks. He wanted to be out here on the sunny hillside with the big dogs. So after that he didn't bark once, though he badly wanted to.

The three dogs soon got the sheep out of the field and down to the stream. Now each sheep had to run across the narrow plank, where Tinker was on guard. The sheep did not want to cross the bridge, and they did all they could to run along the bank. But Tinker was ready for them. He made one sheep go hurrying across the narrow bridge—and then all the others began to go too.

"Sheep love to follow one another," said Dandy with a grin that showed all his white teeth. At first Shadow thought that Dandy was snarling at him, but when he saw his tail wagging, he knew that he wasn't. He wagged his tail at Dandy.

"You see, once you can get one or two sheep going the right way, you can be pretty sure that all the rest will follow," said Dandy.

"I see," said Shadow. "Look—there's a sheep going up the bank!" Off he went, headed the silly sheep back, and it trotted over the bridge with the others.

"Good pup!" said Dandy, and Shadow nearly fell into the water with pride. The sheep ran to the next hedge, with Rafe and Bob behind them. Tinker and Dandy kept them from spreading out sideways, for they had to make them all go through a gap in the hedge.

Shadow helped Dandy all he could, and the sheep went through the gap, jumping neatly across.

"Go with them, young pup, and see if you can keep them in a bunch," said Dandy. So Shadow jumped through the gap too, and ran round the sheep to try and keep them in a bunch for Dandy.

It was hard because there were a great many sheep, and as soon as Shadow had got one right, another would run out, and he would have to get that one back too.

How he puffed and panted, for he was not used to such hard work! Dandy leapt through the gap and watched the puppy doing his best. All the sheep were now in the field, but Shadow was trying his hardest to bunch them.

Bob came up and snapped. "Stop!" he said. "What are you doing? The sheep don't need to be bunched together now. Leave them alone to eat the grass."

"It's all right, Bob. I told him to bunch them just to see if he could!" barked Dandy. "Let them go, Shadow. You've done well."

"Have I done well, please, Bob?" asked Shadow. very anxious indeed to get a good word from the bad-tempered mongrel.

"You're not too bad," said Bob, as he ran to meet the shepherd, who was now coming up the hillside, pleased that the dogs had taken the sheep along so well for him.

"I'm not too bad!" yelped Shadow, in delight, his tail wagging hard. "Bob says I'm not too bad! I'm off to tell Johnny. He *will* be pleased!"

And down the hill ran the little pup, his pink tongue hanging out, and his little heart beating fast with joy. "Johnny, Johnny!" he yelped. "I'm not too bad! Bob says so—and one day I'll be as good as he is!"

CHAPTER FOUR

SHADOW GETS INTO TROUBLE

THE SHEEP-DOG puppy learnt many things from the big dogs on the farm. Dandy, Tinker, Rafe, and Bob taught him how to round up sheep, how to take them where they should go, and how to guide them home when they were lost.

But the shepherd would not let Shadow do very

much alone with the sheep, though the puppy longed to show his little master Johnny, and all the other dogs too, how clever he was.

"Oh, why can't I round up the sheep by myself?" yelped Shadow one morning. "I know exactly what to do. I could round up all this flock and take them to the next field by myself—but Bob won't let me, and the shepherd won't either."

"Be patient," said Tinker. "You may think you know a lot, but you don't. You couldn't possibly take these sheep into the next field by yourself. You are just being silly."

But Shadow was cross, and he watched for a chance to show Johnny and the other dogs just how clever he was!

One afternoon, when he had come back from a fine walk with Johnny, Shadow noticed a small flock of sheep up on the hillside, quite away from the others. He stared over at them, his eyes wide with excitement.

"Just look at that!" wuffed Shadow to himself. "Those sheep have got away! The other dogs haven't noticed. I wonder where they are."

He went to see. Dandy was nowhere to be seen.

He had gone off by himself somewhere. Bob was lying down in the shade of the shepherd's hut, near his master, one eye open, and one ear cocked. He growled when he saw Shadow, and the puppy hurriedly ran away. He was always rather afraid of Bob.

Tinker was scraping madly at a big rabbit-hole and paid no attention at all to Shadow. Rafe was lying asleep in the warm sun.

"Well, look at that now!" said Shadow to himself, puzzled. "Sheep have escaped from the flock and have taken themselves away up there. They may get quite lost. And none of the dogs have noticed!"

He stood and looked at Rafe, wondering if he should wake him. Then a great thought came into his head.

"Bones and biscuits! Here's a chance for me to show what I can do! *I'll* get those sheep down from that field up there myself—and take them to the others!"

As soon as he thought of this, Shadow was running as fast as he could over the green hillside to where the little group of sheep grazed peacefully in a field a good way above the other sheep.

"Now let me think first," said Shadow, as he leapt through the gate. "The sheep are all over there—and before I go to them I must think how I am to take them out of the field. I wonder if there is a gap anywhere. There must be—else how did the sheep get in!"

Shadow ran round the hedges. At the top end of the field he found a small gap. He thought it must be the one that the sheep had found to get into the field.

"Good!" he said. "Now I'll bunch them together and drive them to the gap."

He ran over to the sheep. They looked surprised to see him, but went on eating the grass. Shadow remembered that it was better not to bark too much in case he frightened them and muddled their silly minds so much that they could not be made to do anything.

So he ran first at one sheep and then at another, and soon one big sheep began to run up the field. The others followed. Shadow ran after the first sheep and headed it towards the gap. The sheep did not see it and ran right past.

Shadow felt angry. He tried to make another, sheep go through the gap. "Silly things!" he thought. "Really, it's a wonder they even know how to eat grass! Get back, sheep, get back. Can't you see the hole in the hedge?"

At last one sheep did see it and managed to squeeze through in a great fright. Another followed and another—but the rest ran excitedly round the field and simply would *not* go through the gap! Shadow got very cross indeed and even tried to snap at a sheep's legs—a thing he had been warned not to do.

At last the puppy lay down on the grass, tired out. It was no good! He couldn't get all the sheep out!

"But, tails and whiskers—where did those sheep go that *did* get out!" suddenly wondered the puppy. "I'd better go and look!"

He jumped through the gap and began to hunt for the three sheep. They all seemed to have gone different ways! He put his nose to the ground and sniffed. Yes—one had gone this way—one that way—and the third one another way.

"How tiresome!" thought Shadow. "Now what am I to do? Well, I made them go out—and I suppose I must make them come back!"

He set off after the first sheep, his nose to the

ground. The sheep had gone right to the top of the hill—and over the other side!

"Silly creature!" wuffed Shadow to himself. "No wonder that dogs are needed to look after sheep—whatever would happen to them if they didn't have us to see to them?"

He tore up the hill and down the other side. He suddenly saw the sheep peacefully pulling at some rich green grass in a ditch. Shadow was so angry with it that he ran at it and barked loudly in its ear. The sheep leapt high into the air with fright and scampered off down the hillside, bleating.

"Come back, silly, come back!" barked Shadow. "You are going the wrong way! Oh, do come back. I've got the others to find too!"

But the sheep was too frightened to go back, even though Shadow got ahead of her and tried to turn her. She knew that Shadow was only a puppy and she did not mean to go back for him! She trotted on and on, and the puppy grew frightened.

"What shall I do? I'd better go back and get one of the other dogs," thought the puppy. "Bones and biscuits! Why did I ever try to do this by myself?"

He turned round and ran back up the hillside. Over the top he went, round the hedge, and scampered to where he had left Tinker and Rafe. Tinker was sitting looking rather puzzled, and Rafe was awake now and standing with his ears cocked. Both dogs knew that something was wrong. Bob was growling behind the shepherd's hut.

"Now what's the matter, young pup?" barked Rafe. "What have you been doing?"

"How do you know that I've been doing anything?" yelped Shadow. "But you're right. I've been trying my best to get all those sheep in that little field back to the flock in the big field. I am surprised that none of you noticed they had got away from the flock."

Bob came trotting up, his ears well back. He came right up to Shadow.

"Let me tell you that I had orders from my master this morning to separate those sheep from the others," he said. "That is why they are there. Do you suppose that we should not have noticed something wrong if we hadn't known they were meant to be up there?"

"Oh," wuffed poor Shadow, feeling very silly all

at once. "I'm sorry, Bob—but I've tried to get them back to the others—and three got through a gap in the hedge—and . . ."

The three dogs stared at Shadow in horror. "What!" cried Rafe, "you got three out? Where are they? Did you get them safely back to the flock? What happened?"

"I don't know what happend to two of them," yelped Shadow, his tail drooping sadly. "I followed the third and I couldn't get it back. It is on the other side of the hill. I came to get your help."

Without losing a moment Bob barked some orders to the other two, and they all set off at a gallop, Shadow following behind, trying his hardest to keep up with them. But he was only a puppy, and very tired, so that he was far behind by the time that the others had reached the top of the hill.

Bob ran down the hill. Rafe ran another way, and Tinker went bounding over a rocky piece of ground to find one of the lost sheep. Poor little Shadow did not join in at all. He sat down, his ears drooping, and his pink tongue hanging out. He was very miserable indeed.

"I'm not so clever as I thought I was," he yelped sadly. "What will the other dogs say to me when they get back?"

The more he thought about that, the less he liked the idea. And at last he got up and began to creep down the hill towards the farm. On the way he met Dandy, who was coming back from a long walk all by himself.

"What's up, young pup?" asked the big sheep-dog in surprise, for he saw that Shadow's tail was well between his legs, curled up under his tummy.

Shadow told him everything. "So you see I'm in disgrace," he wuffed sadly. "And I'm just going back to the farm to Johnny, before Tinker, Rafe, and Bob come back and say horrid things to me."

"Well, if you take my advice, you'll stay up here on the hill and hear what they've got to say," said Dandy at once. "No good ever comes of running away from trouble, young pup. Be brave, can't you?"

Shadow stood and thought, his tail drooping. Then he turned back up the hill.

"You're right, Dandy," he said. "I mustn't run

away from trouble. After all, it was my own fault, and I must put up with it."

"Good for you, young pup," said Dandy. "I'll come along with you."

Bob, Rafe, and Tinker had got the three sheep and were making them go through the gap in the hedge by the time that Dandy and Shadow reached them.

"One of us must stay here whilst the shepherd is fetched to mend this gap," said Bob. "Once a sheep knows a hole it will keep getting out of it, and maybe the others will follow. You are silly as a sheep, Shadow! This little crowd of sheep were brought up here, and put in through the gate—and you go and show them a hole to escape from! You'll never be any good!"

"Why couldn't you tell us if you thought anything was wrong?" asked Rafe angrily. "I suppose you think you're so clever that you can do things on your own! Stupid young pup!"

"Go and play with the hens," said Tinker.

"Go and splash in the pond with the ducks," said Rafe. "That's all your fit for. Call yourself a sheep-dog! Why, a cat would do better!"

This was a dreadful thing to say to a dog, and

poor Shadow was very upset and miserable. He put his tail between his legs and began to creep away down the hillside. Then Dandy spoke up for him.

"Well, he may be a very silly little pup, but at least he did stay to get his scolding," he said. "He was running away when I met him—but he came back to hear what you all had to say. He is at least brave, Bob."

The three dogs said nothing for a minute. Then Rafe called after Shadow. "You can come up to us to-morrow if you like, and we'll show you how to get back a wandering sheep. But don't you dare to do anything on your own again till we tell you that you're grown-up!"

So Shadow felt a little happier as he ran slowly back to the farm. "That was a hard lesson to learn," thought the little puppy. "But I'm jolly glad I wasn't afraid to learn it!"

CHAPTER FIVE

SHADOW HAS A FEW ADVENTURES

SHADOW, the sheep-dog puppy, made many other friends besides the dogs. He was an inquisitive little fellow and liked to know everything and everyone. When Johnny was at school, Shadow ran round the farm-yard, when he was not out in the fields, and spoke to all the other creatures.

He knew the hens, especially the big red hen in the coop, whose twelve little chicks ran cheeping in the yard. He knew the two big cocks, and kept out of their way, for they could strike hard with their clawed feet. He knew the waddling ducks, and liked them. They were friendly, and fond of a joke.

The big red hen made a great noise whenever Shadow came near, and at first he was afraid of her. Then he saw that she made the noise, not so much to frighten him, as to call in her chicks.

"You see," explained the red hen one morning, "I can't get out of this horrid coop to call my chicks to me. They are small enough to run out between the bars, but I can't. So when I see danger I cry loudly to them, and they know my call and come running to hide under my wings."

Shadow had been most astonished the first time he had seen the chicks run into the coop. They had rushed there—and then completely disappeared!

Shadow looked into the coop. No—there was no one there but the big red hen, clucking loudly at him, telling him to go away or she would peck his nose and ears.

"I shan't hurt you," wuffed Shadow. "But do tell me where your chicks are? I can't see *one*. Have you eaten them?"

"Eaten my own chicks! What a silly pup you are!" clucked the red hen. "No—my chicks are all here, everyone of them!"

Shadow looked again—and then he saw that the chicks had hidden themselves in the fluffed-out feathers of the mother-hen! One tiny yellow chick peeped from the neck-feathers and two more put out little heads from under a wing. Others peeped from the breast-feathers—and then, as they saw that Shadow was not going to do them any harm, they all crept out once more and ran around the coop.

"It looked as if you had about twelve heads when your chicks peeped out of your feathers!" said Shadow. "Look, there goes a chick out of the coop! Shall I bark at it and make it go back?"

"No, thank you. You would frighten it," said the red hen. "But I wish you could let me out of this coop. I am sure that the farmer's wife has forgotten that I am still shut up here."

"I'll do my best," said Shadow, and he set to work to tug at a loose bar with his strong teeth.

It wasn't long before he loosened it, and the red hen, clucking gratefully, squeezed herself out of the coop.

She took her chicks to the other side of the farm-yard, and then wandered out into the lane with them. There Johnny saw them when he came home from school. He rushed in to his mother.

"Mother! The red hen is out of the coop and she has taken her poor little chicks right out into the lane. They will get so tired and will be lost. Did you let the hen out?"

Now Shadow was at Johnny's heels, of course, for he always met his little master when he came out from school. When he heard Johnny say this, his tail went right down. Tails and whiskers! Wasn't it right to let a hen out of a coop?

Johnny's mother ran into the yard. She saw the loose bar in the coop and guessed that the hen had squeezed past it. Then she ran to find the hen. Sure enough, there she was out in the lane, with twelve very tired little yellow chicks round her.

"You bad hen!" said the farmer's wife, shooing the red hen into the yard. "Take your chicks to your coop. You will kill them if you take them for such long walks before their little legs are strong enough. They are only two days old!"

The red hen was angry. She clucked loudly, but she had to go back to the coop. Johnny nailed back the loose bar. Shadow sat beside him, ears and tail drooping, feeling very miserable. He put his nose on Johnny's knee. Johnny looked at him.

"Yes—I know what you are trying to tell me, Shadow," he said. "It was you who let out the hen! I saw your teeth-marks on the bar. Don't interfere with the other creatures, Shadow. If they are shut up, there's a reason for it. Stick to your own job!"

"Woof!" said Shadow, and his tail began to wag just a little bit. He looked into the coop. The red hen was lying down, her beautiful shining feathers fluffed out all around her. Not a chick to be seen. They were all asleep in her feathers, tired out.

"You might have done a lot of harm, Shadow," said Johnny. "It's a good thing I came home when I did. Now just see if you can do something to make up for that!"

So Shadow looked about for something good to do. But he couldn't find anything at all. The ducks swam on the pond and didn't want any help. The pigs grunted in the sty, and were too sleepy to talk to him. The calves in the meadow ran off when he went near them, and the old cart-horses were too busy even to look at him. Nobody wanted any help. There was nothing he could do.

But the next day something happened. Shadow was running down the lane, nose to the ground, following a most exciting rabbit-track, when he heard a bellowing noise. He looked up in fright, and saw that he was by the orchard where Pincher the bull was kept. And something had plainly made Pincher very angry indeed!

He stood by the hedge bellowing. Shadow saw two boys running off down the lane and he guessed that they had been teasing the bull. He decided that he wouldn't stay there in the lane in case Pincher thought that he, Shadow had something to do with the teasing and tried to get at him.

So he turned to go back to the farm. Pincher caught sight of him and bellowed loudly again. The bull pushed himself against the hedge—and the hedge, which was half-bramble and half-fence there, gave way! Pincher made his way out, and stood in the lane, snorting down his ringed nose.

Shadow looked at the bull. He saw Pincher's horns and knew that they could toss a little dog into the air just as easily as a man tosses a pitch-fork of hay. He heard the bull's bellow, and he was afraid.

He turned to run, and the bull put down his big head and went after him. And then Shadow remembered something. He remembered that a bull in a temper may attack anyone he meets—and Johnny was coming home from the village in a few minutes!

Suppose the bull met Johny! He would go after him and toss him into the air. No—that would never do. Shadow would rather be tossed by a bull himself than see Johnny come to any harm! So the little dog suddenly turned himself round and faced the snorting animal.

"Wooff, wooff!" said Shadow, in his very loudest voice. Then he growled, "Grr-rr-rr-rr-rr! Grr-rr-rr-rr-rr!"

The bull stopped in surprise. He was not used to being faced by anything. Most things ran when he bellowed. He stared at Shadow—and then he ran at him!

Shadow slipped to one side and missed the bull's horns, as Pincher put down his great head to toss him. He snapped at the bull's legs. Pincher hated that. He tried to toss Shadow again, but the brave little dog dodged him cleverly and snapped at Pincher's legs once more, giving him a very nasty nip.

Pincher stood still and thought a little. It was the first time he had been out of the orchard for a long while. He liked the orchard. He felt strange out here in the lane.

Then a train down in the village gave a loud screech. Pincher bellowed at it. Shadow jumped at the bull's swinging tail and bit it hard.

Pincher snorted and turned round. That was just what Shadow wanted! The bull was now facing towards the orchard again. Maybe Shadow could get him on the run and make him go back!

He barked around Pincher. The bull began to move back to the orchard—and then Shadow saw Johnny coming down the lane! He wuffed to him in dismay:

"Don't come near! Go and fetch help! The bull is out!"

Johnny saw the bull. He saw Shadow barking

round him. He knew that it was of no use trying to get the bull back himself, and he hurried to the barns where the men were working, shouting to them as he went. How he hoped that Shadow would be safe! He couldn't, couldn't bear his puppy to be tossed by the bull.

"Pincher's out! Quick! Pincher's out!" yelled the boy. The men came running out of the barn. They took pitchforks and went up the lane. Pincher took one look at them. He wondered if he should charge them and see how many he could toss—but then he saw their pitchforks and he made up his mind that he had better be sensible.

Just at that moment Shadow snapped at his heels. That was too much! The bull gave a bellow of pain and cantered back to the orchard. One of the men had already opened the gate and the bull trotted calmly through it. In a trice the gate was shut and two of the men were mending the gap in the fence.

"Good for you, Shadow!" said Johnny. "You stood up well to old Pincher! I'm proud of you!"

Well, of course, Shadow was as pleased as a dog with two tails, and he wagged his own so fast that it could hardly be seen. More than anything in the world he liked being praised by Johnny. He rushed off to tell the hens, the ducks, the pigs, the other dogs, and the horses.

But they did not mean to make Shadow conceited! Only the little chicks listened in wonder to his tale of the bull. The red hen cackled and told him not to be vain. The pigs grunted and said that *they* were not afraid of the bull! The ducks didn't even bother to listen. They slid into the pond and splashed the proud little puppy as they went.

The big cart-horse listened to Shadow's tale and then stamped his foot hard in a nearby puddle. Mud flew up into the air and fell all over the puppy from head to tail! What a mess he was in!

"What did you do that for, you unkind horse!" cried Shadow, shaking himself well. "You be careful! If I can tackle a bull, I can chase you too!"

The horse whinnied with laughter, and stamped again. Shadow ran away, angry and disappointed. Why were all the creatures so horrid to him just when he had been so clever and brave?

Tinker told him why. "We don't run round

talking about the wonderful things we have done!" he said. "We let others tell about our brave or good deeds, Shadow. You will get vain and conceited if we all listen to you and praise you. After all, you only did what any of us dogs would have done."

"I'm sorry," said Shadow, ashamed. "I won't say a single word more, Tinker. Really I won't."

And he didn't—and then found to his surprise that everyone spoke to him about his adventure with the bull! Well, well—Shadow was learning a few lessons and having a good many adventures. And so long as Johnny was pleased with him, that was all that mattered!

CHAPTER SIX

SHADOW BEGINS TO GROW UP

SHADOW, the sheep-dog puppy, was growing into a big, strong dog. He was a fine creature, with a beautiful coat, big brown eyes, and a tail that seemed to be set on a spring, it was so ready to wag!

He was so big and heavy now that Johnny had

to push him off his feet at night! "You feel like an elephant lying there!" he told Shadow, who at once wagged his tail so hard that he shook the bed from end to end.

"I don't think Shadow should sleep on your bed any more," said Johnny's mother. But Johnny made such a fuss and Shadow looked so dismayed that nothing more was said about it, and the two shared the same bed as before.

As the summer wore on, the big sheep-dogs began to get excited. The sheep-dog trials were soon to be held and the master was going to enter some of his dogs for them.

Tinker, Rafe, and Dandy were all to be entered. Bob was too surly and bad-tempered to be taken to the trials. He sometimes flew at strange dogs without warning, and as there would be many other dogs at the trials, the farmer would not take Bob. So Bob was to be left behind with the shepherd to guard the sheep. He did not seem to mind. He liked doing things on his own.

The farmer did not bother to train the three dogs for the trials. He knew that all that would be asked of the dogs would be the things they were used to doing—rounding up the sheep—taking them to some special place—such things as they did every day.

"They will be timed," the farmer told Johnny. "Those dogs that take the least time in doing what they are told will win. Well—I'd back our three dogs against anyone! Rafe has already won a great many prizes, and I guess he will again!"

Shadow listened to Tinker when he told the growing pup about the sheep-dog trials. How he wished he could enter for them too!

"It is most exciting," said Tinker. "We all go in the car to the hillside outside the next town. That is where the trials are always held. You will meet there dogs from all over the country. My word, some of them are famous, I can tell you!"

"Yes—there's old Jack who has won more trial cups than any other dog in the country," said Rafe. "Even more than I have—and you must just look into the mistress's drawing-room one day, Shadow, and see the prizes I have won. They are all on a shelf in a glass case. Master is very proud of them."

"Why don't *you* have the prizes, Rafe?" asked Shadow. "Can't you eat them?"

"Of course not," said Rafe. "They are silver cups. What a baby you are, Shadow!"

"Are there a lot of people watching the trials?" asked Shadow.

"Hundreds and hundreds!" said Rafe proudly. "You should hear them clap and cheer us. It's our day, you know—our very own day. You should see our tails wag! Mine is so tired when the day is done that I can hardly move it."

"Do you think I shall be able to watch you and Tinker and Dandy?" asked Shadow eagerly. "Is Johnny going? Will he take me?"

"Oh, he is sure to take you if he is going," said Rafe. "It will be good for you to watch the races and the competitions, Shadow, because one day, when you are much older, you *may* perhaps be able to win a prize yourself at the trials. But before you can do that you must practise very hard, be very obedient, and use all your skill and strength to do your job."

"And mind you behave yourself for the next week or two," said Tinker, "or else you won't be able to go and watch *us* winning prizes!"

Well, you should have seen Shadow for the next week! Surely he must have been the best and most obedient dog in the world! He was there before he was called. He knew what Johnny wanted him to do before he said it. He even tried not to lie right on top of Johnny's feet in bed—a very difficult thing for Shadow, because he did so like to be touching Johnny *some*where!

And so you can guess how pleased he was to hear the farmer say to Johnny one morning—"Well, Johnny, you can bring that pup of yours to the trials. He's a good dog, and he won't be any trouble. It'll teach him something to watch what happens."

Johnny was pleased. He brushed Shadow well on the Great Morning. "You will love to watch everything," he told him. "The biggest thing of the afternoon will be when each farmer enters three dogs for one trial—and then you will see how marvellously Tinker, Rafe, and Dandy will work together in a strange field, with strange sheep, in front of hundreds of people!"

"Woof!" said Shadow joyfully, hardly able to keep still. He rushed out to talk to Bob up on the hillside. Bob was not going to the trials, and he pretended not to care anything about them at all.

"Sheep-dog trials!" he growled. "Who wants

to be bothered with such silly things? Isn't it enough that we do our work out here on the hills day by day without having to go and show off to men and women? It's a good thing *I* don't go to the trials—I'd soon show Rafe that I'd go off with all the prizes!"

"You're cross because you're not going, Bob," barked Shadow cheekily. Bob made a snap at him, but the dog was off and away up the hillside. Bob went after him, meaning to punish the youngster, but to his great surprise he could not get near him! Shadow was always ahead of him, and no matter how Bob tried to cut him off and catch him up, he could not come within yards of him.

Bob sat down, panting, his tongue hanging out. Shadow sat down some way off, panting too. He watched Bob out of keen brown eyes to see if he was going to chase him again.

"Youngster, you run very fast," said Bob at last. "You are as strong as ever I have been in my life. You are growing up! Come now—I won't snap at you. Go down the hill with me and run back to Johnny, or you will be left behind."

At the thought of being left behind, Shadow tore like the wind down the hill, his paws hardly seeming to touch the ground. He left Bob far behind. The old sheep-dog looked after him, remembering how he too, once, ran down the hill like the wind. It was good to be young and strong.

Johnny was whistling for Shadow as he ran into the yard. "Come on, boy!" shouted Johnny. "We're all ready. It's time to go."

The farm-wagon was taking everyone. There was the farmer, driving Bess the old mare. There was Johnny's mother, carrying a big basket of food for the day, for they were all to picnic on the hills. There was Johnny, of course, his face red with excitement and happiness. Could anything be nicer than to go to watch sheep-dog trials on a fine windy day up on the hills, with his own dog beside him? Nothing in the world!

The old mare jogged along and the farm-wagon rumbled down the dusty lane. It was the end of August and everywhere was dry and parched. Scarlet poppies danced by the lane-side and blue chicory flowers shone as bright as the sky. Johnny saw them all, as he did each year. They were part of the wonderful day.

It took over two hours to reach the great wide

hillside where the trials were to be held. The sun shone down hotly but there was a fine breeze. Johnny's mother got down from the wagon with the basket of food. Johnny looked at it hungrily.

"Isn't it time for something to eat, Mother?" he asked.

"Good gracious, no! It's only eleven o'clock!" said his mother. Then, as she saw Johnny's disappointed face, she put her hand into the basket and took out some home-made biscuits. "Here you are," she said. "I never knew anyone who could eat at any time of the day or night as much as you can, Johnny!"

Johnny went off with Shadow at his heels. The sheep-dog was so excited at the new sounds and smells and sights that he could hardly keep his tail still. He was thirsty, and Johnny led him to the stream, where the dog lapped for a long time.

"Hie, Johnny!" cried a voice from the crowd that was wandering about on the hillside. "Hie, Johnny! That's a fine dog! It's not Rafe, is it?"

"No. Rafe's over there with my father," said Johnny proudly. "This is my own dog, Shadow. He's not much more than a pup, really, but he looks fully grown."

"My word, he's a fine dog," said the farmer who was looking at Shadow. "Tell me when you want to sell him, Johnny."

"That will be never," said Johnny with a laugh, and Shadow's tail wagged joyfully. Of course Johnny would never sell him, any more than he would ever sell Johnny. As if he could sell anyone he loved!

Shadow met many other dogs, most of them sheep-dogs come for the trials. They were magnificent dogs, strong, intelligent, loyal, and eager to show what they could do. Shadow spoke to some of them very humbly, hoping to learn a few things from these strange dogs from other farms.

They wagged their tails as they answered, for they saw in Shadow one of themselves, and guessed that a time would come when he too would enter for the trials.

It was an exciting walk, that walk on the hillside before the matches began. Johnny showed off his dog to everyone, and if Shadow had not already learnt to be humble instead of vain, he might really have become very conceited by the end of the walk. As it was, he walked back to

Rafe, Dandy, and Tinker with his nose in the air. They noticed it at once.

"Hallo, young pup," said Rafe, jumping at Shadow and rolling him over. "You look as if you think you are the king of dogs this morning. Well, you're not!"

Shadow picked himself up and shook the dust from his coat. "All right, Rafe," he said. "I know I'm not. But really, it *is* nice to belong to someone who thinks as much of me as Johnny does! Anyway, I know I'm not much good compared with you and Tinker and Dandy. I'll bark loudly for you when you win the trials, you see if I don't!"

"All right, young fellow," said Rafe. "Hark—there's the bell for the first entry. I'm in that. It's for speed—and you know how fast I can run!"

Johnny's father whistled to Rafe, who went bounding up to him. He was taken to his starting-point. Away up in the field was a sheep that Rafe was to bring back to the starting-point. There were six other dogs in this trial, each with a sheep to fetch back.

"I hope Rafe wins! I hope Rafe wins!" cried

Johnny, hopping about on one leg in excitement. "Go on, Rafe! Run your fastest!"

A whistle was blown. Each farmer made a short signal to his dog. They raced up the hillside like lightning, beautiful to see in their swift and graceful movements. Each reached his sheep, headed it downhill, and began to take it back.

"Rafe, come on! Come on, Rafe!" yelled Johnny. "Woof, woof, woof!" barked Shadow, Dandy, and Tinker. And Rafe came on, far and away in front of all the others!

CHAPTER SEVEN

AT THE SHEEP-DOG TRIALS

RAFE HAD reached his sheep before any of the other dogs. He fled up the hill as if his paws had wings. The other five dogs were very fast too. Rafe reached his sheep, which was quietly pulling at the grass. It lifted its head as Rafe came up to it, and moved away a few steps. Rafe ran round it and headed it down the hill.

The other dogs did the same with their sheep, but two of the sheep ran the wrong way. Rafe's sheep began to run quietly down the hill, trying to get away from this dog that nosed around its heels.

One of the other dogs tried to make its sheep go too fast, and the frightened creature turned and ran back uphill again.

"Oh, Paddy, Paddy, you hurried your sheep too much!" said the farmer whose dog it was.

Rafe came on steadily. His sheep trotted faster and faster down the hill, not frightened, but determined to leave the dog behind. And Rafe reached the winning post a full minute before the others. He nosed his sheep into a pen and left it.

Johnny shouted and cheered. Good old Rafe! That was another prize for him. Good old Rafe! Tinker and Dandy barked till they were hoarse. Everyone clapped and cheered. Rafe wagged his tail modestly and ran up to his master.

"What a lot of fuss, about nothing!" he barked to Tinker. "A thing we do every day!"

"Yes—but you do it a little better than the rest of us!" said Tinker proudly. "Now look—there's another trial coming on. Dandy and I are in this."

One by one the trials went on. Sheep had to be rounded up in one corner and taken somewhere else. They had to be taken from one pen to another. Sometimes one dog was used, sometimes two. It was marvellous to watch the dogs working with one another, watching each other out of the corners of their eyes, wagging their tails as a signal, barking very rarely, working steadily and well.

Tinker and Dandy did not do as well as the other dogs in their trial. They had one very troublesome sheep among the flock in their pen, and this sheep would not follow the rest.

Tinker and Dandy worked hard at it, but the silly creature turned away from the flock and kept going in the wrong direction.

Johnny groaned. "What a shame!" he said. "That one sheep has spoilt the trial for Tinker and Dandy. They are behind all the other dogs."

"It's not really their fault," said his father. "That sheep is not well, and it is obstinate. It is unlucky for Tinker and Dandy, but at any rate they are doing their very best."

Dandy and Tinker were rather ashamed when they came running back after their match. But

Johnny's father patted them hard, and said, "Well done!" So their tails went up and they began to look forward to the next trial.

"My word, there are some fine dogs here to-day!" said the farmer, as he watched the trials. "Faster than I've seen before, and as sharp as sheep-dogs can be! Look, Johnny—see that dog over there, working with his companion—watch him. He does everything but talk! He is telling the other what to do the whole time, and the second dog is obeying—and yet not a bark passes between them!"

Half-way through the trials, everyone had lunch. How Johnny enjoyed that picnic, sitting on the short green grass, munching at cheese and tomato sandwiches, drinking home-made lemonade, strong and sweet!

His mother laughed at him. "Johnny, I simply can't imagine that you can eat any more! You must have had twelve sandwiches already!"

"No—I've had fifteen," said Johnny. "I counted. Oh, Mother—aren't there any more?"

"Well, I think you will have to stop at twenty," said his mother. "Look—there is some ginger-cake afterwards. Leave room for that."

"Oh, I've stacks of room," said Johnny. "I feel just as hungry as when I began, Mother."

The little party sat on the turf in the hot sunshine, enjoying the strong breeze that blew around the hills. Far away was a thin blue line—the sea. Johnny wished it were nearer so that he might have a bathe.

All the dogs lay stretched out on the warm grass. They were tired after their trials, but they knew that there were still more to come, so they were resting quietly. But Dandy soon got tired of lying still. He was the most restless dog of the company, and could never lie still for very long.

He got up, put his nose down, and ran off after the track he smelt.

"Dandy! Don't go too far!" called the farmer. "The match is beginning again soon."

Dandy wagged his tail. He knew quite well that he mustn't be very long. Down the hill he went, his tail waving happily. Shadow wished he could go with him—but he did not want to leave Johnny. The young dog was happy. It was fun to see the trials—and great to think that one day he would go in for them himself.

Soon the bell rang for the next trial. The farmer got up and looked down the hill.

"Now where has Dandy got to?" he said. "He should be back now. Johnny, can you see him?"

Johnny looked down on the crowd of people and dogs, but even his sharp young eyes could not see Dandy. "I'll go and look for him," he said. "Come on, Shadow."

Off the two went. Shadow put his nose to the ground and smelt Dandy's track. Johnny saw that he had it, and followed him. Down the hill they went—and into the lane—and round the corner—and there they met Dandy.

Poor Dandy! He was limping along in the dusty lane, holding up one of his front paws, looking very sorry for himself.

"Dandy! What's happened?" cried Johnny in dismay. He knelt down in the lane and took hold of the dog's paw very gently. "Dandy! Your paw is crushed and bleeding! What have you done?"

Dandy whined. Shadow listened sadly. Dandy had run down the lane, and a motor bicycle had swerved into him and run over his right front paw. Poor, poor Dandy! Now he would not be able to run in any more of the trials.

"And oh, Dandy! The biggest trial of all is coming on soon," said Johnny in dismay. "The one that takes three dogs working together. Oh, Dandy—Dandy! How you have spoilt things!"

Dandy's tail was down. He was in pain, and was most disappointed to think he could run no more that day. Johnny took him to a stream and bathed the hurt paw. He could not do much else then.

The three of them made their way back up the hill. The farmer saw them coming, and frowned when he saw how Dandy limped. He looked at the dog's paw.

"He'll run no more for a couple of weeks," he said. "Not much damage done—but enough to put him right out of the rest of the trials. And I had set my heart on my three dogs winning the three-dog trial!"

Shadow's tail drooped down with sadness. But suddenly his heart began to beat very fast indeed—for Johnny was saying something most exciting to his father.

"Dad! Let Shadow be the third dog! I know he isn't full grown yet, and doesn't know nearly as much as the others—but he's so sharp, Dad, and so swift. He'll do what the other dogs tell him, I know he will. Wouldn't you Shadow, old boy?"

Wouldn't he! Tails and whiskers, Shadow could hardly believe his ears! Surely the farmer would never let *him* go in for the three-dog trial!

The farmer looked down at the eager little dog. Shadow looked up at him with trusting brown eyes, ready to do exactly as he was told. Tinker barked. Rafe wuffed. Both dogs were willing to let Shadow work with them in the trial.

"Well—I don't see why he shouldn't try," said the farmer at last. "After all, we can't do any worse than lose the match! I've never failed to enter for this trial with three good dogs, and twice we've gone off with the prize. We shall win nothing this time—but at any rate I shall be able to say that I entered my dogs once again."

Shadow was so full of joy and excitement that he could not keep still. Rafe and Tinker spoke to him shortly. "All you will have to do is to watch me and Rafe," said Tinker. "A flick of my eye and you'll know where I want you to go. A wag of my tail and you'll know whether to lie down and wait or come up and help. Use your brains, your swift feet, your eyes, and your good sense."

"Do your best, young pup," said Tinker. "We shan't win—but we'll put up a good show."

The time came. Shadow ran with Tinker and Rafe, so proud that he felt almost as if he would burst. The three dogs had to take a large flock of sheep from a pen, up to another pen at the far end of the field. They then had to separate the sheep into two flocks, and take half of them back to the first pen. The farmer went with them to give orders, for clever as the dogs were, they could not do all this unless they were told.

The farmer shouted a short order. The dogs separated. Rafe went into the pen. Tinker waited at the entrance. Shadow was not far off, ready to do his bit.

Rafe got the sheep out quickly. They came bundling out, frightened and cross. They wanted to spread out over the field, but Tinker was waiting for them. He ran round and round the flock, keeping it together, whilst Rafe kept behind, nosing on the stragglers.

Shadow lay down quietly. His turn had not yet come. He must not interfere with the other two, nor attract the attention of the sheep. But soon one or two sheep edged away from the flock, and up jumped Shadow at a signal from Tinker. His work was to get back any runaway sheep. He must not allow a single animal to leave the flock.

How Shadow worked! How he ran! He watched the sheep, he watched Tinker and Rafe for signals, he watched the farmer for orders. His clear young mind, swift feet, and sharp eyes took in everything—and how he enjoyed it all!

The three dogs got their flock to the top of the field. It was easy to get them into the pen there, for by now the sheep knew that the three dogs were working perfectly together and they sensed that they must do as they were told. Into the pen they went. The farmer stood outside.

He waved his arm. Into the pen went Rafe and Tinker to separate the flock into two. This was really difficult work—and Shadow had difficult work too. He had to keep together in a small flock all the sheep that the other dogs sent outside!

The young dog worked marvellously. He felt sure of himself. He knew exactly what Tinker and Rafe meant when they uttered a short wuff. He felt happier then ever in his life before.

Then back to the first pen went the half-flock of sheep with Tinker and Rafe—and Shadow was left to keep the other half-flock in the second pen. This was easy. He only had to lie down quietly and keep watch.

Everyone cheered and clapped the three clever dogs. Then they watched more dogs doing the same thing—but there was no doubt at all that Rafe, Tinker, and Shadow were the best!

"Those three dogs worked together like one," said the judge, as he gave Johnny's father a great silver cup. "I have never seen such a good team before."

Shadow was beside himself with joy and pride. As for Johnny, he was so proud that tears ran down his face in joy, and he said in surprise, "Oh, Mother! I'm not really crying, but I do feel so very, very happy that I can't help it!"

His mother hugged him and hugged Shadow too. "You both deserve your happiness!" she said. "Good old Shadow! Who would have thought that a funny little pup like you would have turned out to be such a grand big dog!"

CHAPTER EIGHT

A HUNT IN THE HILLS

THE SUMMER passed away and autumn came. Shadow grew into a really big dog. Johnny was very proud of him, and even Rafe, Tinker, and Dandy thought twice before they tried to roll him over now. Old Bob did not take much notice of him—but then Bob took very little notice of any other dog!

Shadow spent a great deal of time running over the hills. He wanted to know every inch of them, because Tinker had told him that that was a thing all sheep-dogs should know—every foot of their own countryside.

"Then if you are told to take the sheep here, there, or anywhere, you will always know exactly where to go and the shortest way to get there," said Rafe. "Don't do what a dog at the next farm did once! He was told to take the flock to a nearby hill—and because he didn't know the way he took them a ten-mile walk, and they were half dead with fright by the time he got them to the hill."

Shadow soon knew every field, every valley, every hill, every glen, and every rock. He knew the streams and where they began. He knew the caves in the next hillside and had been in every one of them. He stored all his knowledge away in his sharp doggy mind.

Winter came on. It was cold up in the hills and snow fell early. The old shepherd was expecting new-born lambs before Christmas, and he lived up in his hut with Bob, the mongrel sheep-dog.

Rafe, Tinker, Dandy, and Shadow went to visit Bob each day, and they felt sorry for the dog on the bitterly cold hillside.

"We have warm kennels," they said. "You have to sleep out here with the sheep."

"Don't waste your pity on me," said old Bob gruffly. "I've lived with my shepherd on the hills all my life. I couldn't bear a soft life like yours. And I like to hear the tiny bleat of a new-born lamb up here in my folds."

"Are there any yet?" asked Shadow.

"Two," said Bob. "Come and see them." He took the four dogs to a small pen. Inside lay a big, woolly mother-sheep, and nuzzling by her were two tiny lambs, whose legs looked far too long for their body.

Shadow sniffed at them through the pen. This was a new kind of sheep-smell—a young smell. He liked it. All smells were good to Shadow. His nose was even sharper than his eyes and ears. When he ran along by the hedge his nose told him that a rabbit had run by there that morning—that a rat was even now close at hand—that a hedgehog had its hole in the bank nearby—that three strange dogs had passed that way—and that all kinds of small birds' feet had hopped and walked under the hedge that morning! Ah, it was marvellous to have a nose like Shadow's!

More and more new-born lambs lay in the folds, or staggered about on unsteady legs. The shepherd was pleased because he had not lost a single lamb. All were strong and healthy, and the farmer was glad. Many new lambs meant much money for his farm.

The weather cleared and the snow melted. The farmer told the dogs to take the sheep to the next hill, where the grass was good. Rafe, Tinker, Bob, Dandy, and Shadow set off, with Johnny behind them, eager for the walk.

The sheep were glad to reach the grass on the next hill. It was always good there. The hill was steep and rocky in places, but the turf was sweet and tasty. Soon the whole flock was peacefully grazing there, with the young lambs frisking beside them.

But after two days a queer change came over the sky. It looked heavy and leaden.

"Almost as if it's going to fall down on top of us!" said Johnny to his father. "Is it going to snow again?"

"Yes," said the farmer anxiously. "And it looks as if it will be a heavy fall too. I think we'd better get the sheep back on our own hill in safety. We can pen them there if we need to."

That was a busy afternoon for the five dogs! The great flock of sheep was scattered all over the hills and it needed all the dogs' swiftness and sharpness to get them together. The little lambs ran with their mothers, bleating in fright.

The flock was moved off down the hillside to the hill where the shepherd had his hut each year, when he waited for the new-born lambs. This was a sheltered hill, and near to the farm.

By the time that the dogs had done their work it was snowing heavily. Enormous flakes floated down from the sky and lay on the grass. Soon the snow was two or three inches thick. The sky was dark, and it was difficult to work in the half-light.

The shepherd stood by the entrance to the pens. He had put up hurdles for the sheep, and he was counting them as they went inside. He knew every sheep and every lamb. He was a marvellous old man, who could smell what weather was coming just by sniffing the wind!

It was eight o'clock and as dark as pitch before all the sheep and lambs were safely in. The dogs were tired out. All they wanted was to lie by a fire and rest, after a good meal. They looked up at the farmer as he swung his lantern for the shepherd.

"All there, Jim?" he shouted.

"There's a big old ewe missing, and the two small lambs," answered the shepherd. "She was always a wanderer, that sheep. She's maybe taken her lambs over the top of the hill and into the next valley. Well—it's too late to fetch her in now."

"Couldn't one of the dogs go?" said the farmer. "I don't want to lose any sheep, Jim. Let Bob go. He's sharp at finding any of your sheep, no matter where they are."

The shepherd spoke to Bob. The dog got up at once and ran into the night. He knew quite well that he must look for the missing sheep.

Shadow got up too. He wanted to help. He was very tired, but he wanted to find that sheep and the two tiny lambs. They were the lambs he had sniffed at through the pen. Poor things, they must be frightened, lost in such a great snow-storm.

Shadow barked to Bob. But Bob had disappeared into the night. Shadow nosed into the snow and tried to smell Bob's track. The falling snow covered everything, even the smell.

"I'll go after him and see if I can catch him up," thought Shadow. "I know the way to the next hill quite well, even when it is covered with snow!"

And now Shadow was glad that he had explored every inch of the countryside, for even when the hills were covered deep in snow he knew his way! He knew when he had come to the big black rock, though it was now white with snow. He knew when he had come to the little bridge over the stream. He knew when he had passed the hawthorn hedge and the great old gorse bush on the hill.

He did not find Bob. He thought that the sheep-dog must have gone another way. Never mind! He would hunt for the lost sheep and lambs by himself. He remembered seeing the old ewe lying down in a sheltered glen the day before. She was a clever one at finding the warmest spots on a cold day. Perhaps she was there!

The dog set off to the glen. He soon came there

and nosed around. But the sheep was not there. Shadow paused and thought again. Where would a mother-sheep take her lambs if she knew that a storm was coming? Sheep were as clever as dogs in some ways, and they could smell the weather from afar.

"The caves!" thought Shadow. "I think she might take her lambs there. She is a silly old wanderer but she does look after her lambs."

He almost lost his way in the snow which was now very deep and soft. The dog found it difficult to make his way round the hill towards the caves, for his paws sank deep in the snow. He knew that he must work quickly, for soon the snow would be too deep for him.

He found his way to the caves. If he had not known every bit of the hillside he could never have reached them, for the hills were now quite different in their blanket of white. The moon came up and the darkness went. Shadow felt a shiver of fright as he saw the world for the first time covered with snow under the pale light of the moon.

He stumbled towards the first cave. Nothing there. He went into the second. Nothing there.

He sniffed towards the third—and tails and whiskers, a strong smell of sheep and lambs came to his nose!

"I've found them!" thought Shadow in joy, and he went into the cave. There, huddled at the back, was the big old sheep with her two small lambs. She did not move as the dog came up to her. She was not going to run out into a strange white world!

"You must come with me!" barked Shadow softly, pushing his nose into her to make her get up. "Come on! You will be snowed up if you stay here. You will starve and your young lambs will die. Come with me before it is too late."

But the old sheep would not move. She was tired and comfortable. Shadow could not make her stir. Outside the snow began to fall again. The dog was almost in despair.

"I wonder if Bob is anywhere near," he thought. "I'll bark and see." So he went to the entrance of the cave, lifted his head and barked loudly over the snowy hillside.

And, not far away, came Bob's answering bark! How Shadow's heart leapt for joy! He barked again—and in a trice old Bob came lumbering over the snow towards the cave.

"I've found the sheep and lambs," said Shadow. "But I can't get the sheep to move."

"I'll soon make her," said Bob. He went into the cave and nosed roughly at the two frightened lambs. They leapt to their feet and ran off to the cave-entrance. They stood there and bleated pitifully.

The mother-sheep at once rose to her feet. She would not stir for herself, but for her two little lambs she would do anything!

After that it was easy for the dogs to push her out of the cave and into the snow. The little lambs kept close beside her.

"Shadow, come this way," ordered Bob. "I know where the snow does not lie so thickly."

The five creatures went slowly over the snow. Bob knew the way as well as Shadow, and the sheep followed obediently.

In about an hour's time they came to the pen on the hillside.

"Well, Bob—well Shadow—so you've brought home the wanderers!" cried the shepherd in joy, lifting his lantern high. "Good dogs, both of you. Ah, you're a fine pair, and I'm proud of you!"

"Good work, youngster," said surly Bob, as he said good night to Shadow. "Good work."

Shadow was happy as he stumbled down the hill towards the farm. He was tired, so tired that his legs would hardly walk—but he had found the lost sheep, and had won praise from surly old Bob. And what would Johnny say when he heard?

In ten minutes' time the dog lay stretched out before a big fire, his head on Johnny's feet. He slept soundly and in his dreams he hunted for lost sheep. Johnny leaned over and patted him. Shadow opened one eye and sighed joyfully. Could any dog possibly be happier?

CHAPTER NINE

SHADOW AND THE NIGHT-HUNTER

IN THE spring-time Shadow the sheep-dog became full-grown. He still felt himself to be a playful puppy, and he gambolled around Johnny as if he were only six months old.

"Stop pulling my shoe-laces undone, Shadow!"

Johnny would say. "Good gracious, don't you know that you are a grown-up dog now!"

The other dogs still treated Shadow as a puppy, though he was even stronger than Tinker. Rafe could still roll him over on the ground. Shadow would bare his teeth at Rafe in play, enjoying the mock-fight.

One day Johnny's father came in with a grave face.

"What's the matter, Dad?" asked Johnny, surprised. "Is one of the cows ill?"

"No. But I've just heard from Farmer Gregory that there's a sheep-killer about," said the farmer.

"Oh, dear!" said his wife. "Are our sheep all right?"

"So far they are," said the farmer. "But Farmer Gregory told me that two of his sheep were killed last night and another one worried so badly that it's no use this morning."

"Oh, Dad! I hope the sheep-killer will soon be caught!" said Johnny. "What is he? A wolf?"

"Shouldn't think so," said the farmer. "I've not heard of a wolf in this district since I farmed here—and that's all my life long! No—it's more likely to be a big dog of some sort."

"Will it be caught?" asked Johnny.

"Caught and shot, I hope," said the farmer. "A killer-dog can do more harm in a few nights than anything else, in a flock of sheep. Well, we must hope it won't come near our flock. Better tell the dogs to lie up on the hills with old Bob and the shepherd, Johnny."

Shadow listened to all this in surprise. It seemed strange to him to think that a dog could ever turn on sheep. Why, surely dogs were the guardians of the silly sheep? Shadow did not know that dogs were kept for other things besides helping a farmer. He ran to talk to the other dogs.

"Do you think it's a dog or a wolf?" barked Shadow.

"Oh, a dog, sure enough," said Bob, baring his yellow teeth. "I'd like to get hold of him. A dog that turns killer is a wicked creature."

"Shall we watch for him at night?" said Shadow eagerly. "Shall I come up here and watch on the hillside with you, Bob?"

"Yes," said Bob. "We'll all watch. We will spread ourselves out around the fields and listen for the killer-dog!"

So for some nights the five dogs lay quietly about the fields, their ears cocked, listening. But not a sound did they hear except for the nightingales singing loudly and an owl hooting over the fields.

But the killer-dog was still at work. From most of the farms around came news of sheep bitten and worried, lambs killed and carried off, and the farmers began to get anxious. They went out into the fields themselves at night, with guns and sticks. But no one ever saw the killer-dog.

"He is a very cunning animal," said Rafe one morning. "He never visits the same farm twice running. He must always know when people are watching for him. Well, we will go on watching too."

They watched each night—and then Johnny told them that for a whole week the killer-dog had not visited any sheep-flocks at all. The sheep had all been safe.

"Dad says that maybe he has been caught in a trap, or has been shut up by his owner," said Johnny. "Anyway, Shadow, you can come and sleep with me again to-night. I do miss you lying on my feet, old son, since you have been watching in the fields at night!"

So that night Shadow went to his old sleeping-place on Johnny's feet, and slept happily and soundly. But in the morning, what a dreadful shock awaited him and Johnny!

The killer-dog had been to the farm, and had killed three sheep! He had carried off a lamb, and bitten two other sheep! Shadow listened in horror.

Johnny's father was white and worried. He could not afford to lose his sheep, for they brought welcome money to the farm.

"Just the night that we called off the watching dogs, the killer-dog came!" he groaned. "Well, I shall go out to-night with a gun—though I am sure he won't come two nights running."

Shadow went off to tell the other dogs, but they knew already, of course, for they had been out with the shepherd.

"We didn't hear a sound in the night," said Rafe, looking rather ashamed.

"I lay out here on the hill with my master, the shepherd, but I saw nothing, heard nothing, and smelt nothing," said Bob. "The killer-dog is the most cunning animal I have ever heard of in my life. He must have slipped along here like a shadow, done his dreadful work, and slipped off again. Oh, if only I could get hold of him!"

Shadow sat and listened, his ears cocked so as not to miss a word. He looked at Rafe.

"The master says the killer-dog will not visit the same farm two nights running," he said. "Rafe, he has not been to Willow Farm yet. Do you think it would be a good idea to go and watch there, instead of here, to-night? Two of us could go, and three could stay here with the shepherd and the farmer."

The older dogs looked at Shadow. Bob wagged his tail. "It might be worth trying," he said. "I and Tinker and Dandy will stay here with the farmer and his gun—and you and Rafe can go scouting round Willow Farm. There is just a chance you may see the killer-dog."

So that night, in the greatest excitement, Shadow slipped out of the farmhouse and went to look for Rafe. Rafe was ready, his tail up, quivering with joy at the thought of a night-hunt. The two dogs raced up the hills like leaping shadows. It was a good long way to Willow Farm, which lay on a hillside to the west, but to the swift-legged dogs the distance was nothing.

They came to the farm. Rafe spoke softly. "Now, Shadow, be careful. The farmer here may be watching for the killer-dog himself, and he may think it is you or me. We don't want to be shot! Choose a ditch or a bank from where you can see the country around, and lie like a fallen tree, quite still."

Shadow did as he was told. He found a high bank under a hedge, and from there he could see plainly all over the moonlit fields, and yet he could not be seen himself. He made himself quite flat, and lay so still that a beetle climbed over his back, thinking him to be a mound of rather hairy grass.

Rafe had disappeared. He was hiding somewhere, watching. Shadow cocked his ears and listened. His nose twitched as he smelt the scents of the night. He watched for two whole hours, and then he became a little bored. It was rather cold on the hillside that night, and Shadow found himself wishing that he was on Johnny's warm feet.

He blinked his eyes. It would never do to go to

sleep. He fixed his eyes on the flock of sheep at the other end of the field. Some were lying down. Some were standing up, pulling at the moonlit grass. A few lambs lay close beside their mothers, asleep.

And then, as Shadow watched, the sheep began to move as if they were frightened. Some ran this way and some ran another. Little lambs bleated. Shadow sprang to his feet. What was going on?

In a trice Rafe was beside him. "He's there!" growled Rafe. "Can you see him? Look—over there, worrying that sheep!"

Shadow looked, trembling with excitement. He saw a big grey-black shadow moving silently among the sheep. It looked like a wolf. Surely it *was* a wolf?

"Now listen," said Rafe. "Together we must attack that killer. He will be strong and fierce, but we must not let him go. He will bite and snap, but you too must do the same, Shadow. You go that side, and I will go the other. Now, be strong and resolute, and we will get him!"

The two dogs separated. Shadow slipped along

the hedge and came out near the great grey-black animal. He sprang at exactly the same moment as Rafe did, and the two of them bit hard at the furry back they landed on. The sheep scattered in terror.

The killer-dog was an enormous Alsatian, so it was no wonder that Shadow had thought him to be a wolf, for he looked very like one. He turned with a snarl as the two dogs fell on him. Then began a fight that all the sheep watched in panic.

Shadow was bitten in the neck. Rafe was bitten on the head and one leg. But the two dogs would not let go of the Alsatian. They clung to him, biting him fiercely, eager to avenge the death of the farmer's sheep.

But in spite of being two against one, the big Alsatian shook off his two enemies, leapt to one side and disappeared into the night. Shadow tried to follow, but he was exhausted and fell down on the grass. Rafe could not run at all because of his bitten leg.

"We've lost him," growled Rafe, licking his leg. "Look here, Shadow, you must follow his trail and find where he hides. If you can do that, maybe we can bring the farmer to his den, and that will be the end of him."

So poor Shadow, tired out, bleeding, and bitten, dragged himself down the field, and followed the Alsatian's trail. It was easy, for the killer-dog was bleeding. He had certainly escaped, but he had taken a great deal of punishment.

For four miles Shadow followed the trail of the killer-dog—and at last it came to an end. The Alsatian had a den in the thick copse on a far hillside. He crept there to lick his wounds. Shadow did not stop for one second, once he had found the den. He stumbled back to the farm, longing for Johnny.

And Johnny guessed at once what had happened. He bathed Shadow's wounds, just as the sun was rising, and then he went to fetch his father.

"Dad! I'm quite sure that Shadow has been fighting the killer-dog!"

"And so has Rafe," said the farmer. "But the dog must have escaped from them."

"Dad, Shadow wants me to follow him," said Johnny earnestly. "I believe he knows where the killer has his den."

"That dog is too clever for anything," said the

farmer, reaching for his gun. "Come on, Shadow. Good dog! We'll follow!"

And Shadow led them to where the great Alsatian lay licking his wounds, in his den hidden away in the copse. That was the end of him. No more would the grey-black shadow go slipping into the sheep-flock, killing, worrying, and snapping. No more would he carry off the little lambs.

"Dad, isn't Shadow the best dog in the world?" cried Johnny, in pride. "Oh, do say he is!"

"Well, so long as Rafe and Dandy and Tinker don't hear me, I'll say it!" said the farmer with a laugh. "Best dog in the world, aren't you, Shadow?"

CHAPTER TEN

JOHNNY GETS INTO TROUBLE

ONE SATURDAY, when Johnny had a holiday from school, he wanted to go nutting on High-Over Hill with the other boys.

"But you can't possibly walk there!" said his mother.

"I could borrow Will's bike," said Johnny. "I

can ride a bike. Let me go, Mother. It will be such fun."

His father looked up from the newspaper he was reading.

"High-Over Hill is dangerous," he said. "I remember your uncle falling down the steep side of it when he went nutting as a boy—and he broke his leg. If you go, you must keep on the west side—that's not dangerous."

"All right, Dad," said Johnny, beaming. "Can I borrow Will's bike, then?"

"Yes, if you take care of it, and clean it when you come back," said his father. "You must remember that if you borrow things, you must always return them clean and in good condition."

"Can I take Shadow with me?" asked Johnny.

"No," said his father. "Shadow has work to do with the sheep this morning—and anyway I don't want him running along the roads all the way to High-Over Hill. It's too far."

"But Shadow wouldn't mind," said Johnny, looking sad all of a sudden, for he hated spending a day without Shadow. "Shadow would like it. Oh, please give him a holiday too, Dad!"

"Shadow is already at work," said the farmer, nodding towards the window.

Johnny looked out. Sure enough, he could see Shadow on the far hill, running with the other dogs, separating the sheep out into little flocks for the shepherd. Some were to go to market that day, and the dogs were helping to bunch the sheep.

Johnny said no more. He had been taught not to argue with his parents. He thought he would get Will's bike, and then he would go up to the hill where Shadow was at work, and explain to him that he couldn't take him with him that day.

Will was one of the farm-hands. He was quite willing to lend Johnny his bike, for the boy was careful. Johnny looked to see if the brakes were all right, thanked Will, and then jumped on the bike. Off he went, cycling up the path that led to the hill where the sheep were grazing.

Shadow came bounding to meet him. He had already seen Johnny that morning, for he had slept on the boy's bed the night before. But when he had heard the shepherd whistling to the other dogs he had licked Johnny's sleepy face, and had run out of the door. He was Johnny's dog—but he had to work for his living just as the other dogs did!

"Shadow, I'm going off for the day," said Johnny. "I'm going nutting."

Shadow looked at Johnny and the bike. He understood quite well what the boy meant. He wagged his plumy tail joyfully. How he loved going off for the day with Johnny!

"Don't look so pleased about it," said Johnny. "I've got to go without you. You can't come to-day, Shadow. I've just come up here to say good-bye to you. I'll be back by tea-time."

Shadow's tail drooped down. All the wag went out of it. What—Johnny was going off without him! He looked up at the boy with mournful brown eyes.

"Don't look at me like that, Shadow," said Johnny, "else I shan't be able to go. You see, Dad says you have work to do to-day. So I can't have you with me. But cheer up—I'll be back by tea-time. I promise!"

Shadow wagged his tail just a tiny bit. He was very sad—but he didn't want to stop Johnny from having a happy day. The shepherd whistled to the dogs, and Shadow had to bound off. He licked Johnny's hand, barked to tell him to be sure and have a good day, and then leapt off to join Tinker and Rafe.

Johnny rode over the hill on his bicycle. He soon joined the other boys, and they shouted to one another.

"Gorgeous day!" yelled Ronnie.

"What have you got for your lunch?" shouted Harry. "I've got ham sandwiches, and the biggest bit of chocolate cake you ever saw."

"Have you all brought baskets for the nuts?" said Johnny. "I've got one. I hope I get it full. My Dad loves hazel nuts. He eats them with salt."

The boys rode off together happily. It was a long way to High-Over Hill, but it was quite the best place for nutting. There were hundreds of fine nut-trees there.

One of the boys got a puncture in his back tyre. All of them jumped off to help. Johnny found a puncture-mending outfit in the saddle-bag at the back of his bike, and very soon the puncture was mended.

Then off they all went again, chattering and

shouting. When they came to the place where they meant to go nutting, they jumped off their bicycles, laid them on the grass, and ran to the trees.

"Golly! I never in my life saw so many nuts before!" cried Harry eagerly. "Just look at them! My word, they are beauties! Let's pick some to have with our lunch, shall we? Then we can set to work properly after that, and fill our baskets."

The boys plucked the clusters of nuts. What fine ones they were! Then they sat down and undid their packets of sandwiches and cake. How they enjoyed them! Most of them had brought something to drink as well. Then they ate their nuts. Harry had actually brought a pair of nut-crackers, which everyone voted a very clever thing to do. But some of the boys, who had very strong teeth, preferred to crack the nuts in their mouths.

"All very well for *you*," said Harry, cracking his nuts with the crackers. "But my teeth aren't very good—and I'm not going to risk breaking them, I can tell you."

After lunch the boys took up their baskets and went nutting. Some of them had sticks with crooked handles so that they might pull down the higher branches.

Harry went over the top of the hill. He gave a shout. "I say! The trees on this side are marvellous. What about picking some of the nuts from here?"

But the other boys were too busy picking from the other trees, so Harry went to join them. Johnny was doing a funny thing. He hadn't a stick to pull down the high branches—so he fetched his bicycle, and propped it up against a nut tree, and now he was standing on the saddle so that he could reach the fine clusters above his head.

When he had picked all he could see, he left his bicycle under the tree and went to the top of the hill. He just wanted to see over, down the other side. And, of course, when he got there, he spied the trees that Harry had seen, so full of nuts that the branches hung almost to the ground. The hillside was very steep, and nobody had dared to risk getting the nuts from the trees there. So there were hundreds and hundreds.

Johnny forgot that he had been told not to pick nuts on the steep side of the hill. His eyes shone with delight as he thought of how he could fill his basket to the brim with enormous nuts. He began to climb down the steep side of the hill towards the clump of hazels.

The earth on the hillside was loose. Stones rolled down as Johnny scrambled along. Then he slipped and clutched at a tuft of grass. But the grass was not strong enough to hold him, and came out by the roots. Johnny fell headlong down the hill, bumping into rocks and stones as he went, trying to clutch at trees and bushes, but just missing them.

He fell with a crash to the bottom, hit his head on a stone and then lay still, with his eyes closed. He had not shouted, because he had been too frightened, so the other boys did not know he had fallen.

Harry and the others picked nuts steadily. The boys were spread out well on the other side of the hill, and nobody missed Johnny. They all thought he was somewhere with them. It was only when it was time to go home that they missed him.

"It's four o'clock," said Harry. "We'd better be starting back. Let's get our bikes. Anyway, we can't possibly get any more nuts into our baskets or our pockets either!"

Every boy had his basket full, and his pockets too. They were very pleased with their afternoon's work. They picked up their bicycles and were about to jump on them, when Harry looked round in surprise.

"Where's Johnny?" he said.

Johnny was certainly not with them. Harry shouted loudly. "Johnny! Johnny! We're going now! Hurry up!"

There was no answer. Then Ronnie spoke in surprise. "He must have gone home, because his bike isn't here! There are only our bikes—not Johnny's. He must have slipped off before us."

"So he must," said Harry. "Well, what a funny thing to do! He might have waited! Come on. We must hurry now."

Off went the boys, whistling and chattering, never knowing that Johnny's bike was under a hazel tree where he had left it—and that Johnny himself was lying with his eyes still closed at the bottom of High-Over Hill. Nobody worried about him at all.

Nobody? Yes—there was somebody worrying dreadfully! And that was Shadow. Shadow loved Johnny so much that he knew when things were going wrong with him. And poor Shadow was sitting anxiously on the hillside at the farm, watching and watching for a boy who didn't come. What was to be done about it?

CHAPTER ELEVEN

GOOD DOG, SHADOW

SHADOW SAT and waited, his eyes turned towards the lane down which Johnny should come. Rafe ran up to him.

"What's the matter? Why is your tail down?"

"I'm unhappy," said Shadow. "I feel that something is wrong with Johnny. I know there is!"

Rafe knew what Shadow meant. He looked towards the lane too. "Maybe Johnny will come along soon," he said. "Perhaps his bicycle has broken."

"I wish Johnny wouldn't go out without me," said Shadow. "I can look after him when I am with him."

Rafe sat down to keep Shadow company. Dandy came up too, and the three dogs sat together in silence. Then, at five o'clock, they saw Johnny's mother come out of the farmhouse and look up the lane to see if Johnny was anywhere about.

"Johnny! Johnny!" she called. "Are you back yet?"

Will came by, carrying a pitchfork over his shoulder. "I don't think Master Johnny's home yet, Mam," he said. "He said he'd bring my bicycle as soon as he got in, because I wanted it myself this evening—and he hasn't come."

"Oh, dear! I wonder what has happened," said Johnny's mother anxiously. "It's past tea-time now—and Johnny promised to be home."

Shadow darted down the hill and ran up to Johnny's mother. He looked up at her with dark, worried eyes.

"So you are anxious too," said the farmer's wife. "What has happened to Johnny, Shadow? Can't you find him for me?"

Shadow barked and then whined. If only he *could* find Johnny!

He ran to Rafe. "Where is High-Over Hill, where Johnny has gone?" he asked. "Have I ever been there?"

"No," said Rafe. "But do you remember where we once took some sheep to Farmer Langdon? Well, High-Over Hill is just past here—you can see it when you pass the farm—a great big hill sticking up into the sky."

"I shall find it," said Shadow. "But what a long way it is! Good-bye, Rafe. I don't know when I shall be back."

Shadow set off. He did not go the way that Johnny had gone, up the lane and along the road. No—Shadow knew the short-cuts among the hills. He ran along swiftly, smelling the well-known scents of rabbit, fox, weasel, hare, and stoat as he went. How he wished he could suddenly smell Johnny too!

It was a long way to Langdon's farm, even by the short-cuts. But Shadow did not once think of being tired, although he had done a hard day's work. All his mind was full of Johnny. He must find Johnny. He must, he must. He knew in his faithful heart that Johnny was in trouble. Something had happened to Johnny. He was sure of it.

He came at last to Langdon's farm. The sun was setting. It would soon be dark. Shadow trotted quickly down the lane past the farm. He did not dare to take the short-cut through the farmyard itself, because the farm-dogs would set on him. No dog allows another on his own farm without the farmer's permission.

Some way ahead, outlined against the evening sky, was High-Over Hill. Shadow ran even more swiftly. Something told him that Johnny was there.

The dog ran up the slope of the hill—and suddenly his heart beat quickly. He could smell Johnny's scent! Johnny had been there, no doubt about that.

The dog nosed about the trees—and suddenly he found Johnny's bicycle, leaning against one of the hazels. He sniffed at it. Then he nosed about to find the boy's footprints. He found plenty of them, leading here and there. Shadow followed them with his nose—and at last he found footprints leading to the top of the hill.

Shadow followed them. He came to where Johnny had begun to climb down the hill—he came to where Johnny had slipped and fallen—and then, on the breeze, there came such a strong smell of Johnny that Shadow lifted his head and barked loudly:

"Johnny! I'm here!"

And a feeble voice answered from the bottom of the hill: "Shadow! Oh, Shadow!"

Shadow leapt down that hill in a trice! He cared nothing for stones and rocks. Only one thing filled his heart and mind—he had found his beloved little master again. Johnny! Johnny!

In two seconds the big sheep-dog was beside the boy, licking his hands, his face, his legs, anywhere that he could find to lick. He whined as he licked Johnny, and the boy put both his arms round the big dog's neck.

"Oh, Shadow! I'm hurt and I've been so frightened and lonely here all by myself. Oh, Shadow, I did want you so! How did you find me? Shadow, don't leave me."

Shadow sat down beside Johnny. He was happy

again now that he had found his master. But he was worried too. How could he get help for Johnny without leaving him? He couldn't get anyone if he didn't leave Johnny to fetch help. Yet the boy was so frightened and lonely. Shadow could not bear to leave him. His head was bleeding too. Shadow licked the bad place gently to make it clean. The boy curled up close to the dog for warmth, for he was very cold.

Shadow lay as close as he could. He could feel Johnny getting warmer and warmer. That was good. It was getting dark now. Shadow heard Johnny's breathing and knew that he was asleep. Perhaps he could leave the boy for a short while and go to Langdon's farm for help?

He slipped gradually away. Johnny was tired, and still slept on. Shadow ran round the hill and went to the farm. The farm-dogs set up a tremendous barking. The farmer came into the yard to see what the noise was about. Shadow ran to him and tugged at his coat.

The farmer flashed his lantern down and saw the big sheep-dog. "Why if it isn't Johnny's Shadow!" he cried in amazement. "What do you want here, Shadow?"

Shadow barked and ran to the farm-gate. The farmer knew at once that the dog wanted him to follow. He went back to the farmhouse and fetched a coat. Then he set out behind Shadow.

"Don't go so fast!" he called. "I can't see my way as well as you can!"

But Shadow was impatient to get back to Johnny. Suppose the boy had awakened and had missed him? How upset he would be!

Soon he and the farmer were beside the hurt boy. Johnny awoke and shivered, puzzled to see the lantern shining down on him. Then he groaned because his head ached so badly.

"Well, old son, so you've had a bit of a fall, have you?" said Farmer Langdon. "I'll carry you back to my farm. Your dog fetched me. Ah, he's a marvel, that dog of yours!"

"He found me," said Johnny. "Oh, I was glad when I heard him bark. It was the nicest sound in the world!"

The farmer carried the boy gently back to the farm. Mrs. Langdon bathed his head and his ankle, which had been badly sprained. Then she telephoned to his mother to tell her what had happened.

"We'll keep him here to-night," she said. "He is quite all right now, except for a bad head and a swollen ankle. We've got Shadow here too."

"*Shadow!*" said Johnny's mother in astonishment. "How did *he* get there? He didn't go with Johnny to-day."

"Well, he found him at the bottom of High-Over Hill," said Mrs. Langdon. "He came to fetch my husband, and that's how we got Johnny! He's a wonderful dog."

"Dear old Shadow!" said Johnny's mother, her eyes full of tears. "I don't know what we would do without him."

Johnny stayed at the farm that night, and slept in the spare room there, with Shadow, as usual, stretched over his feet. It was the first time that Shadow had slept in another house, but he didn't mind where he slept so long as he was with Johnny. The boy was taken home the next day, and his mother hugged him. His father welcomed him too, and the boy told him how the accident happened.

"I disobeyed you, Dad," he said. "But I didn't mean to. I quite forgot what you had said about not going over the steep side of the hill. But I've been well punished for it. And if it hadn't been for Shadow, I don't know what would have happened to me!"

"Good dog, Shadow!" said Johnny's father, and he patted the big dog. "Good dog! I'll let you off your work for two or three days so that you can be with Johnny whilst he is getting better. Look after him, won't you?"

Of course Shadow would! It was the thing he loved best in the world.

CHAPTER TWELVE

JOHNNY AND THE BIG BOY

JOHNNY WENT to school each day. He walked down the lane, past one or two farms, and then up a lane to the hill on which his school stood.

The school-bell rang each morning to warn the children to be in time. Johnny hated being late, and so far he never had been. But then an astonishing thing happened. He was late every day for a week!

"What is happening to you, Johnny?" asked his teacher in surprise. "You can't go on like this. Why, you have always been so early—and now you are late each day!"

Johnny said nothing. He did not want to tell tales. It was not his fault that he was late. It was all because of the big boy who had come to work on the farm next to Johnny's.

This boy was fifteen, and big for his age. He was trimming and cutting the hedges that ran round the farm—and one morning he had spied Johnny running along to school.

He thought it would be fun to tease the boy. "I'll make him late for school each day," thought the big boy. "He'll get into trouble then!"

So he called to Johnny. "Come and talk to me!" he ordered.

"I can't," said Johnny. "I shall be late for school."

"What does that matter?" said the big boy. "You come here and do as you are told."

But Johnny didn't come—so Tom, the big boy,

jumped down from the hedge-bank and caught hold of him.

"I'll show you what happens to boys who don't do what I tell them!" he said. He pushed Johnny through the hedge and rolled him over on his back. "Now you just lie there and say your six-times table to me," he said. "If you make a mistake you'll have to begin all over again."

Well, Johnny wouldn't, of course. He struggled hard to get away, but Tom was very strong indeed. It was quite easy for him to hold Johnny down with one hand. Tom kept an eye open for the farmer, in case he came along—but usually he was at the other end of the farm at that time of the morning.

In the end poor Johnny had to say his six-times table. Tom said that he got it wrong, although he didn't, and made him say it all over again.

The school-bell stopped ringing. "I shall be late now," said Johnny, scrambling up. "You are a mean thing. I hope you cut your hedge all wrong and get into trouble!"

Tom aimed a blow at him and missed. Then he went on with his hedge-cutting, grinning to himself every now and again when he thought of Johnny being late for school.

He looked out for Johnny again the next morning. But Johnny was on the look-out for Tom too! If Tom had not hidden quietly behind the hedge, so that Johnny didn't see him until he was right on top of him, the small boy would not have been caught. However, just as he thought he was safe, out pounced Tom and caught him.

"Now you can say your *seven*-times table this morning!" said the unkind boy, putting Johnny down on his back and standing over him. "Go on—say it."

And that was how it was that Johnny was late for school all one week. No matter how he tried to slip along to school without being caught by Tom, he couldn't seem to. The only other way to school was a very roundabout way, and that would make the boy late for school as well.

Johnny was sad and worried. He did not like to tell anyone about Tom, because he hated telling tales. But he told Shadow.

"I just can't *help* being late, Shadow!" he said. "That big boy, Tom, always stops me on the way to school. I do wish you could come with me and stop him."

But Shadow couldn't, because he was always at work at that time in the morning. He thought about it and a plan came into his doggy mind. He knew that all the farm-hands stopped work at twelve o'clock for dinner. Well, Shadow was free then, too, and so were the other dogs. He would punish big Tom then, and make him sorry he had ever teased Johnny.

Shadow told the other four dogs what his plan was. They wagged their tails and agreed to help. Shadow kept his eye on Tom that morning as the boy moved about the next farm. At twelve o'clock he was working on the ditches not far from Johnny's farm. Good!

When twelve o'clock came, Shadow barked to Rafe, Dandy, Tinker, and Bob. The sheep were safe on the hillside. The shepherd was going back to his hut for his dinner. For a little while the dogs were not wanted.

They raced off to where Tom was putting down his tools, ready to go to his dinner too, which he always had at the farm. The dogs surrounded the boy as he turned to walk down the field.

"Hallo!" he said, in surprise. "What's all this? What have you dogs come for?"

Rafe and Shadow sat down in front of Tom. Dandy sat at the back. Tinker and Bob sat one on each side. They did not wag their tails—but neither did they show their teeth. At least, not just then!

"Well, I never saw dogs behave in such a queer way before," said Tom, puzzled. "What do you want? I've nothing for you!"

The boy walked a few steps, but a growl from Shadow stopped him. He looked at the big sheep-dog.

"Now look here, just you let me pass," he said. "You've no right to come and act like this. I've never hurt any of you in my life! Let me pass!"

Shadow growled again. Tom tried to go to the right, but Bob growled so fiercely that he did not dare to move a step. Then the boy tried to slip past Tinker, but the big sheep-dog bared his teeth in such an alarming manner that he did not dare to move.

The dogs moved in a little closer. Tom looked at them in despair. This was dreadful! Such a thing had never happened to him before, and he simply didn't know what to do about it. He suddenly shouted loudly:

"Help! Help!"

But there was no one to hear him. The dogs growled so fiercely when he shouted that he did not like to shout again. He didn't know what to do. He tried once more to break out of the ring of dogs, but it was no use. He was afraid of being bitten.

So in the end Tom sat down and waited for the dogs to go. They went at one o'clock when they heard the shepherd whistling for them.

Tom made his way to the farmhouse, angry and hungry. The farmer's wife was cross. She had cleared away dinner. There was none for Tom.

"You'll have to go without, she said. "You don't suppose I'm going to wait a whole hour for you, do you? What in the world have you been doing?"

Tom told her about the dogs. The farmer's wife laughed. "I'm not going to believe a tale like that," she said. "You must see you are in time to-morrow—or no dinner for you!"

But Tom was not in time the next day either—

for Shadow played exactly the same trick on him. And this time Johnny saw them! He was going along by the hedge and to his enormous surprise he saw Tom sitting down in the middle of a ring of dogs, looking angry and puzzled.

"Whatever's happening?" cried Johnny, climbing through the hedge. "Shadow! Rafe! Dandy! What do you think you're doing?"

And then the boy suddenly knew! Shadow had planned to make Tom late for his dinner—just as Tom had made Johnny late for school. Johnny stared at Tom.

"These are my dogs," he said. "They are playing a fine trick on you."

"I know," said Tom sulkily. "Call them off."

"Not till you promise not to make me late for school any more," said Johnny.

"I'll do what I like," said Tom.

"All right," said Johnny. "I'll not call off the dogs then. Good-bye."

"Wait a minute—wait a minute!" called Tom. when he saw Johnny moving off. "I can't miss my dinner again. I'm jolly hungry."

"Well, you know what to do then," said Johnny. "You've been mean to me—and now you're being paid back. It serves you right. If you want me to call off my dogs now, you'll have to say your twelve-times table!"

So Tom had to stand in the middle of the listening dogs and say his twelve-times table. And although he was fifteen years old, he made three mistakes in it!

"You'd better go back to school," said Johnny. "Now just see you don't lie in wait for me any more—else my dogs will pay you a visit again! Come, Shadow—come, Rafe! Here, boys!"

The dogs bounded after him, and they all went back to the farm together. Tom didn't make Johnny late for school again—and Shadow got an extra big pat for being so clever!

CHAPTER THIRTEEN

JOHNNY AND THE GYPSIES

SHADOW HAD grown into a big and beautiful collie-dog. His head was sleek and shining, his ears were always cocked, and his plumy tail was so ready to wag that it was always quivering.

Johnny was prouder of Shadow than of anything else he owned.

"Are you prouder of him than of your new clockwork railway?" asked Harry, in surprise. Harry had no railway, not even a train, and he thought Johnny's railway track and train were the finest he had ever seen.

"How can you ask me such a silly question!" said Johnny, pulling Shadow close to him. "Why, Shadow is alive and can play with me. He loves me and I love him. A railway track isn't alive, and though I like it awfully, I can't love it! Don't you love your dog, Harry?"

"Well, I haven't got one that is exactly my own," said Harry. "We've plenty of dogs on our farm—but they all seem the same to me."

"You just get a puppy of your own, and then see how you feel about dogs," said Johnny. "Why, I couldn't possibly do without Shadow—could I, Shadow, old chap?"

Shadow wagged his tail hard. He was glad that Johnny couldn't do without him. He knew quite well that he couldn't possibly do without Johnny!

Shadow was now cleverer than any of the other dogs at working with the sheep. The shepherd was always praising him.

"I thought Rafe was a marvel," he said to the

farmer, "and Dandy is as swift as the wind. Old Bob does wonders too—he really understands every word I say—and Tinker is the strongest dog I've ever had. But that Shadow! He is a wonder dog. You want to watch him with the sheep nowadays, sir. You'd be surprised."

So the farmer went to watch, and the shepherd put Shadow through all the work he knew. He sent him to fetch one special sheep, and Shadow brought it in at once. Then the shepherd told him to take it to a certain wood not far off. Shadow stood looking up at the shepherd, his tongue hanging out, his tail wagging, his bright eyes shining.

"Well, go on then, boy," said the shepherd. "I expect you think I'm mad this morning, making you do these things just for show—but I'm proud of you, you see."

So Shadow took the sheep to the wood, and then returned it to the flock, unfrightened. That was the best of Shadow. He could make the sheep do anything he wanted them to do—and yet not even the smallest of the lambs was afraid of him.

"I've left my coat over the other side of the hill," the shepherd said to the farmer, without looking at Shadow, who had come up to him for further orders. Shadow wagged his tail.

"It's a nuisance," said the shepherd, still speaking to the farmer. "I want that coat."

Shadow darted off at once. The farmer looked at the shepherd. "You don't mean to say he's gone to fetch it just because he heard you telling *me* about it?" he asked in astonishment. "Why, you didn't even look at the dog!"

"I tell you, you don't need to say anything to that dog—he just knows what you want and goes to do it," said the shepherd. "You'll see—he'll be back with the coat in his mouth in half a second!"

It was certainly more than half a second before Shadow appeared over the top of the hill, but it could not have been more than two minutes!

He bounded up to the shepherd and laid the coat down at his feet.

"Look at that!" said Andy. "He had the sense to roll the coat up before he carried it. He knew it would drag on the ground and stop him from getting back quickly, unless he could keep it from tangling up his legs. I tell you, he's a wonder dog!"

The farmer was just as proud of Shadow as

Johnny and the shepherd. He talked about him as he went from farm to farm, and soon the whole countryside knew about the clever collie-dog, Shadow.

And it was all because of that, that something happened to Shadow.

A tribe of gypsies suddenly appeared in the countryside, and asked Johnny's father for permission to camp on a meadow near a stream.

The farmer would not allow them to. "No," he said; "last time I let gypsies camp on my land, they stole my hens and set fire to a fence. You can't camp on my farm."

The gypsy who had come to ask permission scowled at the farmer. He was a dark brown man with black curly hair, curious gleaming eyes, and bright gold earings in his ears. He turned on his heel and went away without a word.

But that night, when Johnny went walking with Shadow through the meadows, what did he see but five or six gypsy caravans camping in the very place where his father had said they must not camp!

"Hie!" cried Johnny indignantly. "Didn't my father say you weren't to camp on his land?"

"Is this his land?" asked a gypsy, putting on a surprised face.

"You jolly well know it is!" cried Johnny. "You'd better get off it quickly. My father always means what he says!"

The gypsy walked near to Johnny, and his face was frowning and ugly. Shadow growled.

The man stopped. "You'd better not come any nearer," warned Johnny. "Shadow will fly at you if you do."

The gypsy stared at the dog, and a sharp look came into his eyes. "Is that the dog everybody talks about?" he asked.

"Maybe," said Johnny. "*You'll* talk about him too, if he gets his teeth into you! He doesn't like the look of you at all. Down, Shadow, down!"

Shadow had leapt up at the man, who stepped back quickly.

"Call your dog off," he said. "I kill any dog that goes for me!"

"Shadow won't be killed by a gypsy!" said Johnny scornfully. "He's too quick. Now, you'd better get your camp away from here pretty quickly, before my father comes along."

The man scowled again and went back to the camp, taking a last look at Shadow as he went. Johnny whistled to Shadow, and the two of them went home.

"Dad, the gypsies are camping on our land after all," said Johnny that evening. "I told them to go. The gypsy I spoke to pretended that he didn't know it was your land."

"Well, they'll know to-morrow all right, if they are still there!" said the farmer shortly.

Next morning the camp *was* still there, and the farmer took Shadow and Rafe and went to speak to the gypsies.

"Clear off my land before noon," he ordered. "Do you understand me?"

"Yes," said the same man who had spoken to Johnny the day before. "But you'll be sorry for this!"

"Oh! So you think you'll do some damage before you go, do you?" said the farmer at once. "I know you gypsies! Well, I'll leave someone on guard—and anyone who tries to damage my crops, my hedges, or my fences, will be very sorry for themselves."

He whistled to Shadow, who came bounding

up. "Shadow! Guard this place! See that no gypsy harms anything belonging to me!"

Shadow looked up at the farmer's stern face. He wagged his tail. He understood very well what he was to do. He could do it, too! Woe betide any gypsy who tried to injure the farmer's property! He would have Shadow to reckon with.

The farmer went off with Rafe. Shadow sat down near the caravans. His sharp eyes took in everything. He saw the dirty children, the smelly caravans, the line of half-washed clothes, the fire on which an old gypsy woman was cooking something that smelt very good.

The gypsy-man went to the old woman and spoke to her. She nodded, and looked at Shadow.

The gypsy had told her to poison a lump of meat and throw it to Shadow. She slipped inside her caravan and took down a bottle. She went back to the fire, and took out a tasty lump of rabbit-meat with a sharp stick. She opened the lump and poured some drops from the bottle into the juicy meat. She closed the meat together and laid it on the ground for a few minutes.

Then she threw it to Shadow, expecting the dog to gobble it up. But Shadow did not move. He was not going to accept any gift from the enemies of his master! He did not even turn his nose to sniff at the meat!

"It's no good," said the woman. "He won't even look at it!"

The gypsy-man took a quick look round. Then he picked up a stone and threw it hard at Shadow. The dog was looking at some gypsy-children and did not dodge aside as he certainly would have done if he had seen the stone coming.

It hit him hard on the side of the head. It was a big stone, and the dog rolled over at once, half stunned. He felt as if he were in a dream. He could not move. His head hurt him dreadfully. Then he gave a sigh and shut his eyes. It was safe for the gypsy to go to him now, for poor Shadow could do nothing to help himself.

"Quick! Get a sack and put him into it whilst he's like this!" said the gypsy to the old woman. Onc or two more gypsies came running up, and soon the big dog was pushed into a large, strong sack. The gypsy tied up the neck with rope, and then he and another man carried poor Shadow to their caravan. They threw him inside and shut the door.

"Now we'll clear out!" said the gypsy with the earings. "I told the farmer he'd be sorry he told us to go—and he will! I can sell that dog for a good price!"

CHAPTER FOURTEEN

SHADOW, WHERE ARE YOU?

JOHNNY WENT to school as usual that morning after saying good-bye to Shadow, who came to the farm-gate with him.

"I'm taking him with me when I go to speak to those gypsies," his father had said to him. "They won't like the look of Shadow and Rafe at all!"

"I'd be sorry for anyone who tried to get the better of a sheep-dog!" called back Johnny. "Good-bye, Dad! See you at dinner-time!"

After morning school Johnny walked back home. He kept a look-out for Big Tom, the boy who had once lain in wait for him and teased him. But Big Tom had had his lesson, and now he did not even look at Johnny as he went by.

Johnny watched for Shadow to come and meet him from school. The sheep-dog always knew when Johnny should be home, and if he possibly could, he went to meet him. He was nearly always at the farm-gate—and when he saw Johnny he would go bounding up the farm-lane to meet him.

"Really, you would think Johnny had been away for a whole month, the way that dog greets him!" Johnny's mother said.

But this morning there was no Shadow. Johnny was surprised. Could Shadow be working up on the hills with the other dogs? He did not think so, because it was not a busy time for the shepherd. Besides, the other dogs could do any work needed just then.

"Funny!" said Johnny, feeling quite hurt.

"Shadow *always* comes to meet me. Shadow! Shadow! Where are you?"

Johnny whistled. He had a very piercing whistle that he had learnt from his father. It echoed all round the farmyard, and Tinker, Dandy, and Bob up on the hills heard it too.

"He's whistling for Shadow," said Bob. "Where *is* old Shadow?"

"Rafe said that the farmer left him to see that the gypsies did no damage," said Tinker. "But they've gone now. Where has Shadow got to, I wonder? He hasn't been up here this morning."

"Oh, I expect he is seeing the gypsies safely out of the county!" said Dandy.

Johnny went indoors. He found his mother making butter in the dairy.

"Mother! Where's Shadow?" he asked. "He didn't come to meet me this morning."

"Didn't he?" said his mother in surprise. "Well, I really don't know where he is. Your father said he had left him to guard the gypsies. He took Shadow with him, I know, and Rafe too—but he only had Rafe with him last time I saw him. He'll be in to his dinner in a minute. Ask him if he knows where Shadow is. Don't look so worried!

Shadow is probably up on the hills playing with the other dogs!"

"He isn't, I'm sure," said Johnny. "He never, never misses meeting me from school, if he isn't working, Mother."

"Well, he's over by the gypsy camp, I expect," said his mother.

"He may be," said Johnny, "but I can't see any camp now. It looks as if the gypsies are gone. Mother, can I go and see?"

"Not now," said his mother. "It's almost dinner-time. Look, there's your father."

The farmer came in with Rafe at his heels. He stamped the mud from his shoes. Johnny ran up to him.

"Dad! Where's Shadow?"

"I left him guarding the gypsies," said the farmer. "Hasn't he come back? Well, the gypsies are gone, so Shadow will be here any minute now. I gave the gypsies till noon to clear out—and I saw their caravans moving off about an hour ago."

Johnny's heart sank. If the gypsies had gone, there would be no need for Shadow to remain at the camp. Then where could he be?

"Mother, I simply *must* go over to the place where the gypsies camped and just see if old Shadow is still there," he said. "You see, he might be waiting there till Dad gave him the order to come away. You know what a faithful old thing he is."

"He's cleverer than to wait there when the gypsies have gone!" said the farmer. "You won't find Shadow hanging about the camp now these rascals have gone! He'd see them safely off my land, and then he'd come back to the farm. Maybe he's around somewhere."

"Dad, I've called and whistled and whistled and called," said Johnny, in despair. "If he was anywhere within a mile he'd hear me and come! You know how sharp his ears are. Something's happened to him."

"Nonsense!" said his father. "He'll come popping his sharp nose in at the door soon. You sit down and eat your dinner!"

"Please mayn't I go to the gypsy camp first?" begged Johnny, almost in tears.

"No," said his father. "You'll have time enough afterwards. Come, don't be a baby!"

Poor Johnny had to sit down and try to eat. He

couldn't swallow anything! He tried his best to, but it made him feel sick. He went very pale.

"Johnny! What's the matter with you?" asked his mother at last. "Don't you feel well?"

"Not very," said Johnny, quite truthfully. "I can't eat any dinner, Mother."

"Leave it then," said his mother. Johnny put his knife and fork together thankfully. He slipped down from his chair and went outside. He felt better when he was in the open air.

"Shadow, you always know when there is something wrong with *me*!" he said out loud. "Well, *I* know when there is something wrong with *you*! And I feel it now. You're in trouble. You wouldn't have stayed away from me all this long time if you could come to me. Where are you, Shadow—where are you?"

But no pattering feet sounded on the farmyard cobble-stones. No welcome bark echoed from the hills. There was no dog to be seen anywhere, except old Jessie, the farmyard dog, Shadow's mother. She ran up and licked Johnny's bare leg.

"Jessie, don't *you* know where Shadow has gone?" asked Johnny miserably. He set off to the meadow where the gypsies had had their camp. It took him about ten minutes to get to it. There was now no camp to be seen. All the caravans had gone. Only the marks of their wheels showed where they had stood.

Johnny stood and looked round at the camp. He saw the place where the gypsies had had a fire. He saw the bits of paper flying about that they had left. He saw two or three opened tins in a ditch. But there was no sign of Shadow.

Johnny walked round the deserted camping-place—and then he suddenly stopped and stared. At his feet was a large stone—and sticking to it were some hairs! Johnny picked up the stone. He looked closely at the short brown hairs.

"Those are Shadow's hairs!" he thought, his heart sinking down to his boots. "I'd know Shadow's brown and yellow hairs anywhere! Oh, the wicked men! Dad left Shadow to watch them—and they threw this stone at him. They must have stunned him."

Poor Johnny stared at the stone as if he could not believe his eyes. He felt quite certain that he was right in what he thought. His legs felt suddenly as if they would not hold him up, and the boy went to sit down on a fallen tree-trunk. Near it was a lump of meat.

Johnny looked at it. Why hadn't the meat been eaten by one of the half-starved dogs belonging to the gypsies? He picked it up and smelt it. There was a curious smell inside it.

"I bet it's poisoned!" said Johnny to himself. "This is worse and worse. Thank goodness Shadow had the sense not to touch it. I suppose they tied up their own dogs so that they wouldn't eat it—and when they went they left it behind, hoping that one of *our* dogs would gobble it up and die! Oh, Shadow—where can you be? Have the gypsies taken you away?"

Johnny was so unhappy that he didn't know what to do with himself. "I'm not going to school this afternoon," he thought. "I'm going to find out where the gypsies went. I'm going after them! If they've got Shadow, I'll find out somehow, and rescue him. Shadow, I'll get you somehow!"

CHAPTER FIFTEEN

JOHNNY HAS AN ADVENTURE

JOHNNY TOOK one more look round the gypsy camp and then went back to the farm. His father had gone back to his work. His mother was lying down, resting.

"I won't disturb her," thought Johnny. "And I'm sure if I told her I was going after the gypsies she would say I must wait till Dad had finished work this evening, and let him go to. But by that time it might be too late. I must go now."

Johnny did not like to ask Will if he would lend him his bicycle, as he sometimes did. He was afraid that Will would want to know why. So he decided to walk. He wondered if he should take one of the other dogs.

"I rather think I will," he said. "He might be useful to me. I'll take Tinker. He loves a walk."

So he whistled to Tinker, who was lying down asleep on the hills. Johnny had a special whistle for each of the dogs. Tinker pricked up his ears when he heard the whistle. He knew it was for him.

"There's Johnny whistling for me," he said. "I must go. I wonder what he wants."

He bounded off down the hillside, proud that Johnny should whistle for him. Johnny usually only wanted Shadow!

Johnny was waiting for him, his face grave and solemn. "Tinker, the gypsies have taken Shadow!" he said. "They hit him with this stone—look! They must have hurt him dreadfully. I want you to help me to get him."

Tinker sniffed at the stone. He smelt Shadow's scent at once. He looked up at Johnny, his tail down. He knew that the boy was worried and unhappy.

"Come on," said Johnny. "We must go before anyone misses us."

The two slipped out of the farm-gate. Nobody saw them except the hens and the pigs, and *they* took no notice at all.

Johnny went up the lane and then turned off to where the caravans had come out of the meadow. He could see the marks of the wheels quite well.

"We can follow these until we come to the main road," he said to Tinker. "Then we shall have to ask which way the caravans went, because the marks of their wheels won't show there."

The boy and the dog went along the lane, watching the wheel marks of the vans. When they came out on to the main road, it was as Johnny had said—there was nothing to tell them which way the caravans had gone.

Johnny saw a man working in the ditch at the side of the road. He called to him.

"I say! Which way did the gypsy caravans go? Did you see them?"

"Yes. They went along towards the next farm," said the ditcher. "Five or six of them."

"You didn't see a sheep-dog with them, did you?" asked Johnny eagerly.

"No, I didn't," said the man. "I only saw one or two half-starved creatures that came nosing around my coat over there, looking for my dinner!"

"Thanks," said Johnny. He and Tinker set off down the road. Soon they came to where the road forked into two, and again Johnny did not know which way to go. He looked about for somebody to ask. There was nobody.

"Bother!" said Johnny. Then he saw a little girl peeping over a wall at him. He called to her.

"Little girl! Did any gypsies go this way?"

The little girl was very small. "What are gypsies?" she said.

"Oh, people that look awfully dark," said Johnny. "They live in houses on wheels."

"Oh," said the little girl. "Yes—I saw some funny houses on wheels go by before my dinner-time. They went down there."

She pointed down one of the roads. Johnny smiled at her.

"Thanks," he said, and set off again. He and Tinker hurried on for a mile or two—and then Johnny's heart beat fast! In a field to the right of him he saw the gypsies' caravans.

"We've caught them up!" he said to Tinker. "Now, we must be careful. We don't want to be seen. The gypsies know me."

The boy and the dog bent low behind the hedge as they came near the caravans. The vans were all pulled up in a field near a stream, for the gypsies liked to camp near water for the sake of their horses.

Johnny peeped through the hedge. One of the dogs heard him and cocked up its ears. It barked loudly. The gypsies looked round. They could not see Johnny or Tinker because they were hidden by the hedge.

"Oh, Tinker! How ever are we going to get near the caravans without the dogs barking at us?" whispered Johnny desperately. "I think we'll have to wait till night comes."

The boy made himself a kind of bed in the ditch. and Tinker cuddled down beside him. He knew quite well what Johnny meant to do. He would sleep there with one eye open until it was dark! Then he and Johnny would creep through the hedge to see if they could find Shadow.

Johnny could see through a gap in the hedge. He watched the gypsies unharness their horses and take them to the stream. He watched the children playing round the caravans. He heard the women talking to one another, and he saw one of them make a fire and light it. The smoke came over the hedge.

"Tinker, it's very funny—all the caravan doors are open except one," whispered Johnny. "I bet that's the one they've got poor old Shadow in! Oh, how I wish I dared go right up to it and open it and find out!"

But Johnny was afraid of the men. He lay in the ditch with Tinker and waited for darkness to come. He felt thirsty but not hungry. Tinker crept out once and went to a puddle and drank some rain-water. Johnny wished he could do the same!

Darkness fell early. Johnny got out of the ditch, feeling stiff and cold. He found a big gap and pushed his way through. He could see the gypsies gathered round the camp-fire, eating a meal. The dogs were with them, gnawing at the bones thrown to them.

Johnny moved without a sound to the caravan whose door was shut. He was just about to go up the steps when one of the men saw him by the light of the fire.

"Who's that?" he shouted. Johnny didn't answer. One of the gypsy boys ran up and caught him.

"What are you doing here?" he cried. Then he let go quickly because Tinker jumped at him and growled. The gypsies' dogs came running up then.

"Oh, Tinker! We must do *something*!" cried poor Johnny, not at all liking the look of the thin, half-starved dogs who were baring their yellow teeth at him.

But Tinker didn't care tuppence for the dogs. He sprang at one and rolled him over. The other fled, barking madly. The first one jumped up and fled away too.

"Good!" cried Johnny. He turned to face the watching gypsies. "Where's my dog Shadow?" he cried. "You threw a stone at him and hit him. I know you did. Then you caught him and took him away. Where is he? He's in this caravan, I'm sure!"

"You are quite wrong," said one of the men, his gold ear-rings shining in his ears. "We have no dog except those you saw."

"Well, let me open the caravan door and look inside!" said Johnny.

"That would be no good," said the man. "Your dog is not there. We are not thieves."

But just then Johnny heard a sound that he knew very well indeed! It was a whine—and it was Shadow's whine, too! It came from the shut caravan.

"That's Shadow whining!" cried Johnny, and he was up the steps in a trice. The gypsies ran to stop him—but Tinker was on the steps too, snarling and growling so fiercely that the men cowered back, afraid.

Johnny opened the door and looked into the dark caravan. He could see nothing. "Shadow! Shadow! Are you there?" he cried, expecting to see his dog come bounding up. But no Shadow came. Instead, loud barks came from a heavy sack at the back of the van, where poor Shadow was still imprisoned.

Johnny whipped out his pocket-knife. He cut the rope that tied the neck of the sack—and Shadow leapt out at once. He licked his little master from head to foot, he put his paws up on Johnny's shoulder, he whined with excitement and happiness.

"Oh, Shadow—dear, dear Shadow!" said Johnny almost crying for joy. "Are you hurt? Let me feel you all over!"

But there was no time, for the gypsies were shouting outside the caravan, and Tinker was howling madly. Someone had thrown a stone at him and hit him on the nose and he was fiercely angry—but he did not like to fling himself on the gypsies unless Johnny told him to. Johnny ran to the door, with Shadow beside him. He faced the camp.

"I've two fierce dogs with me," shouted the boy. "If you dare to throw one stone at us, or stop us leaving this camp, I'll set both dogs on you!"

The men stood back sullenly. They were terrified of the big sheep-dogs. Both the dogs were snarling in a most terrifying manner, and they kept close to Johnny to protect him. All three passed out of the field-gate untouched. The gypsies shouted rude things after them, but Johnny didn't mind that! Hard words broke no bones!

Tired, cold, hungry, but very happy, the boy walked home with Tinker and Shadow. Shadow kept close to his heels, adoring the boy who had saved him. When Johnny's hand swung back, Shadow gave it a quick lick, that made Johnny smile to himself in the darkness.

His father and mother were very anxious about him. Johnny stumbled into the farmhouse tired out—and stammered out his story. His mother set a plate of soup and toast in front of him and made him eat.

"Poor Johnny!" she said. "Never mind—it's all come right. Shadow hadn't much of a bruise on his head—I've bathed it well, and it will soon heal. Smile and be happy, Johnny."

"Mother, I *am* happy!" Johnny said. "I'm only tired and cold—but I'm very happy. I've got dear old Shadow back again. Oh, I was so worried about you, old chap!"

Shadow sat as close to Johnny as he could get. He and Tinker had had a good meal. Tinker had gone back to the other dogs, but Shadow was going to sleep on Johnny's bed as usual!

And you can guess how glad they both were to feel one another so near that night! If Johnny's mother hadn't forbidden it, I really believe Shadow would have got right under the sheets with his beloved little master!

CHAPTER SIXTEEN

THE HORRID LITTLE DOG

SHADOW the sheep-dog bounded into the dining-room one morning, and found the family sitting talking.

"I didn't get nearly as much money for my lambs as I had hoped," said the farmer. "That means we shall be short of money for a while. I wish the hens were doing better."

"Yes, I wish they were too," said Johnny's mother. "But they have gone off laying, and I am only getting about a quarter as many eggs as I should be getting. I wonder what we can do about it."

"You can have all the money in my money-box," said Johnny, at once. "I was going to save it up for your birthday, Mother—but if you need it, you can have it. I *was* saving up for something else too—but that can wait."

"What was that?" asked his father.

"Well, I don't know if you've noticed Shadow's collar," said Johnny. "It's almost falling to bits! He does badly need a new one. I wanted to get him one of those smart ones—with big brass studs round it. But if you'd like my money, he can wait for that."

"Oh no. You keep the money," said his mother, smiling. "It is very sweet of you to offer it, Johnny, but I think we can manage without your savings, old son."

"We'll think of something, don't worry," said the farmer. He patted Shadow on the head. "You shall have your new collar! You're worth quite a lot of new collars, Shadow!"

But all the same Johnny didn't spend his money on a new collar for Shadow. He spent half of it on his mother's birthday, and bought her a bottle of lavender water, which she always loved. The rest of the money he put back.

"You see, Shadow," he said, "it might just happen that Mother *did* need the money—so we'll keep it just in case—and you'll have to wait for your fine new collar. I haven't nearly enough for it, anyway. They cost a lot of money, you know."

Shadow wagged his tail and looked up at Johnny. He didn't care whether he had a new collar or not. Whatever Johnny said or did always seemed exactly right to him.

"All the same, Shadow, you look rather a disgrace with *such* a very worn-out collar," said Johnny. "The shepherd has just bought Bob a fine new one. I expect you feel quite sad when you see him wearing it, and then think of your dreadful old one."

Shadow jumped up at Johnny and put his paws on the boy's shoulders. He licked his nose. He wanted to tell him not to worry about old collars. Johnny understood and laughed. He rubbed Shadow's nose.

"You just try and think of some good way of earning money for us," he said.

Shadow couldn't think of any way at all, and neither could Johnny. But Johnny's mother thought of one. She told Johnny about it.

"I've had a letter from an old lady called Miss Robins," she said. "She wants to come here for a holiday, Johnny, and she will pay me for coming. The money she gives me will help us nicely. Isn't that lucky?"

"Oh, yes," said Johnny. "I'll try to be as quiet as possible, Mother. I know old ladies don't like a lot of noise."

"She has a dog of her own," said Mother. "I hope he will get on all right with all the farm-dogs."

"Well, they are not around the farmhouse much except Shadow—and Jessie, the farm-dog," said Johnny. "I'll keep Shadow out of the way till Miss Robins gets used to him."

Miss Robins arrived the next week. She was rather a stern-looking old lady, tall and thin, and she walked very upright, rather like a soldier. Johnny felt a bit afraid of her.

She carried her dog in her arms. It was a small, smooth-haired fox-terrier, about six months old. As soon as it saw Johnny it yapped at him.

"He doesn't like you," said Miss Robins. "I hope he soon will."

Johnny thought it was a pity that Miss Robins didn't let her dog go on a lead and walk. He was sure that the puppy hated being carried. Shadow came up to have a look. The fox-terrier nearly flung himself out of the old lady's arms, trying to snap at Shadow.

"Oh, dear—I hope your dog won't go for mine," said the old lady. "He is such a big dog, isn't he? I don't like big dogs."

"Come away, Shadow," said Johnny, feeling angry. After all it was Miss Robins' dog that had snapped at Shadow! Johnny felt that he wasn't going to like either the old lady *or* her dog!

Miss Robins liked the farm. She liked the good farm-food—the golden butter, jugs of cream, home-made cheese, and rich milk. She liked the the comfortable-looking hens and the waddling ducks.

But she didn't like the other dogs! One morning Rafe, Tinker, Dandy and Bob all came down to the farm together to see Shadow—and the old lady heard her little dog, Spot, barking madly. She rushed out to see what was the matter—and found all four of the big sheep-dogs staring in surprise at the bad-tempered little terrier. Bob sat down to look at him. He had never seen such a cross little dog before.

"Get out of my yard!" the fox-terrier barked. "Who are you? How dare you come here? Get out or I'll fly at you!"

Shadow trotted up and spoke to Spot. "Don't be foolish. This is *our* farmyard, not yours. And don't bark and snap at bigger dogs than yourself. You'll be sorry one day if you do. You may be thankful that we are all good-tempered dogs!"

"I don't think I like this yapping animal," said surly Bob. "I think he had better go."

"He can't," said Shadow. "He belongs to an old lady who is living here."

"I don't belong to her! She belongs to me!" barked Spot indignantly.

"Well, why do you let her carry you about then?" asked Shadow in disgust. "You might be a doll or a teddy-bear, the way you snuggle under her arm when she goes for a walk. Don't you like walking? "

"If you are rude to me, I shall tell my mistress and she will tell the farmer's wife to keep you all away from the farmhouse," barked Spot fiercely.

"You're a silly little fellow," said Rafe, baring his big teeth at Spot. "Behave yourself, or I'll nip your ears."

He snapped at Spot—just as the old lady came out to see what the noise was about. She rushed at Spot at once and picked him up. "You bad dog!" she scolded Rafe. "Fancy going for a dog so much smaller than yourself! I shall complain to the farmer about you. Be careful you don't get the whip!"

Rafe stalked off in disgust. The whip! What was the old lady talking about? Didn't she know that sheep-dogs were never whipped? The other dogs followed him.

"What a stupid little creature that dog is!" said Tinker. "If only he knew how to behave himself he could have had some fun with us. As it is I shall give him a nip whenever I can—just to teach him to be polite to his elders!"

So Spot didn't have a very good time, and had to keep his eyes wide open all day long in case one of the farm-dogs was lying in wait for him.

He was a quick little dog and could easily get out of the way. He soon discovered all kinds of things. He found out where Shadow's dinner was put down and often ran to it before Shadow was there, and ate half before the big sheep-dog came up. Shadow was very angry.

He went to find Spot to punish him—but that clever little dog was always safely on his mistress's knee, and Shadow did not dare to snap at him there.

Then one day Spot went for a walk with Miss Robins on the hills—and they came to the shepherd's hut.

Spot ran inside, sniffing in delight. What a lot of lovely smells there were there! The shepherd's heathery bed smelt fine. His coat smelt good. It was hanging on a nail. There were smells of the other dogs too. Spot enjoyed himself very much.

And then he came across the shepherd's dinner! It was in a paper packet. It didn't take Spot long to tear it open. Inside there were meat sandwiches and cheese. Spot gobbled up the whole lot! He licked his lips—that was really delicious!

He slipped out of the shed. Rafe, who was nearby, saw him—and smelt the smell of meat and cheese. He ran after Spot at once, guessing that the naughty little dog had stolen the shepherd's dinner.

But Spot was too quick for him. He tore after his mistress, who was picking flowers on the hillside, and whined pitifully to her.

"Poor little dog!" she said. "Are you tired? Come to Mistress then!"

She picked him up—and of course Rafe could not possibly give him the nip he had meant to give him.

"Coward!" said Rafe to Spot. "You wait till I catch you alone, that's all! Horrid little thief!"

The shepherd was very angry when he found that his dinner had been eaten. He had not seen Spot up on the hillside, and he quite thought that it must have been one of the sheep-dogs. He was really shocked, for he had felt certain that all the dogs were honest and well-trained.

He called them to him and scolded them well. They sat round him, ears down, and tails quite still. They hated to be scolded, especially when they knew that they had done nothing wrong.

"We'll punish that horrid little Spot!" said Tinker fiercely. "Shadow you follow him about and see if you can't possibly get him alone. Bring him to us and we'll show him what happens to thief-dogs!"

"I'll do my best," promised Shadow. "That dog is just as much a nuisance to us as Miss Robins is to poor Johnny! She is always scolding him for whistling and singing. He hardly dares to open his mouth!"

CHAPTER SEVENTEEN

SPOT GETS INTO TROUBLE

SPOT KNEW quite well that the other dogs were angry with him, and he was afraid. He was a spoilt, petted little dog, and he certainly had not needed to eat the shepherd's dinner, for he got far too much to eat from his mistress. She was always giving him chocolate and sweet biscuits, and things that were bad for a puppy.

"You are disgustingly fat," said Shadow to Spot, as he passed near to where Miss Robins was sitting in the farm-garden, Spot close beside her. "One of these days you will find that you are too fat to run—then you won't be able to run away fast enough when we all chase you. Greedy little dog!"

Spot barked rudely at Shadow. He always felt quite safe when he was with his mistress. She adored him and would have kept off half a dozen dogs if they had dared to attack him whilst she was near.

Shadow lay down nearby, keeping an eye on Spot. He meant to get him alone if he possibly could. Spot went on and on barking at the big sheep-dog. Miss Robins bore it as long as she could, then she called to Shadow.

"Go away! Can't you see that Spot doesn't like you?"

Shadow cocked up his ears to listen—but he didn't move. He put his head down on his paws again and stared at Spot. Miss Robins got very angry.

"*Will* you go away when I tell you to, you disobedient dog! I shall call Johnny if you don't."

Still Shadow did not move. Miss Robins heard Johnny whistling not far off and shouted to him.

"Johnny! Johnny! Your dog is making himself a great nuisance! Come and make him go away. And do stop that awful whistling! It really gets on my nerves."

Johnny stopped whistling. He opened the farm-garden gate and went inside. He saw Shadow lying quietly down and heard Spot barking madly.

"My dog doesn't seem to be doing anything," said Johnny politely. "After all, he has just as much right as Spot in his own farm-garden."

"Don't talk to me like that," said Miss Robins sharply. "And, dear me, what a dirty little boy you are this morning, to be sure! Just look at your jersey! It is covered with black marks—and what a dreadful hole you have in the right sleeve! Really, you look a ragamuffin! Can't you go and clean yourself up?"

"Well, I'm cleaning out a cow-shed," said Johnny. "It's no use wearing good clothes for that. I keep this old jersey for dirty work. I wouldn't have come to talk to you in it, only you called me."

"Really, your dog and you are just about as untidy as one another!" said Miss Robins. "Shadow wants a good brush—and look at his collar! It is almost falling off his neck. If you care for your dog at all, you should really buy him a new one. One day it will fall off altogether, and then you will have to pay a fine for keeping a dog without a collar."

"I have already brushed Shadow to-day," said Johnny patiently and politely, "but he has been working up on the hills, and rolling about in the heather. As for his collar, I am saving up to buy a new one. But they are rather expensive, you know."

"Well, call him to you, for goodness' sake," said the old lady crossly. "Really, what with Spot barking in my car for ages, and your great untidy dog lying down there staring at me and at poor Spot, I feel quite cross."

Johnny felt cross too. But he knew that he must never be rude to people older than himself, so he said nothing more to the old lady. He whistled quietly to Shadow, who jumped up at once and followed him. Johnny went to the gate and opened it to go out. He felt very much inclined to bang it hard—but that would be rude and silly. So he went out quietly, hearing bad-tempered little Spot still barking his head off.

"I wish he *would* bark his head off!" thought Johnny. "Then perhaps he wouldn't be such a nuisance!"

Shadow kept his eye on Spot for the next day or two, but that little dog was too smart to give him a chance to catch him. So Shadow decided that he had better hide himself somewhere. Then, if Spot couldn't see him, maybe he would run out alone—and Shadow could follow him and catch him. So Shadow hid in the pig-sty, and put his eye to a crack to watch if Spot went out alone.

And the next evening, Spot did! He was tired of being with Miss Robins, who had petted him really too much that day. So he waited until she had gone to talk to the farmer's wife—and then he slipped out of the farm-gate and made his way down towards the duck-pond. He thought it would be great fun to bark at the ducks.

Shadow saw him going. He slipped out of the pig-sty, kept close behind a hedge, and followed

Spot. Spot ran along happily, sniffing here and there. He was enjoying himself. It was nice to be on his own.

He came to the duck-pond. The ducks swam peacefully on it. Spot stood on the bank and barked.

"Wuff, wuff, wuff!" He barked as loudly as he could, and the ducks fled to the other side of the pond in fright. Spot was delighted. He tore round to that end of the pond and barked again. He didn't see Shadow slipping up behind him.

"WOOF!" said Shadow suddenly in Spot's ear. The little dog turned in fright. He saw the big sheep-dog standing nearby, stopping his way of escape. He whined in fear.

"No good whining for your mistress now," said Shadow. "You're caught!"

But Spot wasn't going to be caught! He suddenly thought that he could easily swim across the duck-pond to the other side, and escape that way. So he jumped, splash, into the water, and worked his puppy-legs to swim away.

But alas for Spot! When he got near to the middle of the pond, his legs got caught in some weeds. They pulled him down. He sank. His head went below the water and he began to splutter and choke.

Shadow watched in surprise. What was happening? Why was Spot behaving so queerly? Why was he going down under the water? The big dog was puzzled.

Spot came up to the surface, gasping. He whined in fear, and then sank again, spluttering. Miss Robins, who had been looking everywhere for him, came running up to the pond.

"Oh, Spot, Spot! You're drowning!" she cried. She stepped into the water, meaning to try and save him. And then Shadow guessed what was happening and jumped in to save Spot!

He didn't think about how horrid the little dog had been. He didn't think that it would be a jolly good thing if the old lady tried to rescue him and got herself muddy and wet. He just saw something he could do, and he did it. He swam right to the middle of the pond and put his head down to look for Spot.

He found him at last, caught fast in the weeds. Shadow got his teeth into the little dog's collar and jerked at it. Spot came up to the top of the water with a rush. He worked all his legs madly, half drowned. Shadow did not leave go. He swam steadily towards the old lady, dragging Spot along with him. He put him safely on the bank and then shook himself well.

Thousands of silvery drops flew from his thick coat all over Miss Robins. But she did not even notice them. She knelt down by Spot, patting him, and trying to get some weeds out of his mouth.

"Poor little dog!" she kept saying. "Poor little dog! That's right! You're almost better now."

Spot soon felt almost all right. He got to his feet and looked at his mistress. Then he looked at big Shadow, still shaking the wet from his coat. He ran over to him and jumped up at him. He licked the big dog with his pink tongue.

"Thank you, Shadow, thank you!" he barked. "You are a good friend. I didn't deserve your kindness—I know that. But if you will give me a chance, I'll show you I can be a better dog. Thank you a thousand times!"

The old lady saw Spot thanking Shadow, and she went to Shadow too. She patted him with tears in her eyes.

"You are a good, brave, kind dog," she said. "I

know you don't like my darling Spot—and yet you saved him. I shall buy you a grand new collar!"

Shadow wagged his tail politely. He didn't like Miss Robins and he was sure she would forget. He ran off to tell the other dogs what had happened.

"Well, of course, you couldn't possibly leave even a horrid little dog like Spot to drown," said Rafe. "As for his promise to be better, I don't believe it."

"Well, we'd better give him a chance," said Shadow. So they gave him a chance—and to their great astonishment Spot kept his word. He didn't bark at them any more. He didn't steal their biscuits or their dinners. He was very polite to them, and asked them all kinds of questions, as if he really and truly did want to learn from them.

"He's not a bad little fellow, really," said Rafe three days later. "If he goes on like this, I've half a mind to let him come round the farm with me. I could teach him a lot. Has the old lady bought you the new collar she promised you, Shadow?"

"No," said Shadow. "But perhaps she will. I heard her telling Johnny how I had saved her precious Spot—and she said she had ordered the best collar in London for me."

Well, sure enough, the best collar arrived! And what a marvellous one it was! It was dark brown, and had a shining buckle. It had big brass studs all the way round. When Johnny saw it he stared in the greatest delight.

"Good gracious! I've never seen such a beauty, never! Thank you, Miss Robins, very much indeed. I do like it—and Shadow will look simply fine!"

He did—and didn't he feel grand when he went to show the other dogs!

"You deserve it, Shadow," said Johnny, who was with him. "You really do. You didn't like Spot any more than I did—and yet you did your best for him. It's funny—I like Spot now, and I like Miss Robins too. I'm sorry they are both going soon. You could have taught Spot a lot!"

"We've taught him plenty!" barked Shadow. "He's a much, much nicer dog now!"

CHAPTER EIGHTEEN

THE RUNAWAY LAMB

ONE DAY Johnny was really excited. He went to find Shadow to tell him the news.

"Shadow! Come here and listen! Dad says that you and I can take a flock of sheep to market for him to-morrow. All by ourselves! What do you think of that?"

Shadow was sitting on the ground, listening.

Thump, thump, went his big tail on the grass! It was nothing to Shadow to take sheep to market —but it was a great thing to Johnny because he had never been allowed to do such a thing by himself before.

"You see, the shepherd's ill," said Johnny. "So Dad is taking his place up on the hills—and I'm to take Dad's place and go with the sheep to market. Uncle Harry will be there to meet us, and we hand over the sheep to him."

Thump, thump, went Shadow's tail again. A long day with Johnny! What fun! They would be doing a job of work together, and both of them would be proud, and how they would enjoy being together! So often Shadow had to work up on the hills with the other dogs, and Johnny had to go off to school. It was a real treat to be able to spend a whole day with one another.

"We'll take our dinner with us," said Johnny, making plans in excitement. "I'll take a fine bone for you, Shadow, and some of your favourite biscuits. We'll turn the sheep on to a hillside whilst we have our dinner together. Will you like that?"

"Woof!" said Shadow, in his deep dog-voice

He jumped up at Johnny, put his paws on the boy's shoulders, and gave his cheek a very wet lick.

"Shadow! What a wet tongue you've got to-day," said Johnny, getting out his handkerchief. "Now you be ready with the sheep at nine o'clock to-morrow morning and I'll come along and meet you."

Shadow knew which sheep had to go to market. He had heard the shepherd counting them out the week before. These sheep had been put into a pen by themselves. There were sixteen sheep and four well-grown lambs.

The farmer called Shadow the next morning. He hardly had to say a word to the dog, for Shadow knew exactly what to do. He tried to push open the hurdling that acted as a gate to the fold.

"Now, now—you are getting too clever!" said the farmer, with a laugh. "At least let me open the fold for the sheep to come out!"

As soon as the way was open, Shadow ran into the fold. He got the sheep out quickly.

"Take them down to Johnny," ordered the farmer. "Now you use your sense to-day,

Shadow. See that Johnny gets them all to market!"

Shadow wagged his plumey tail. Of course he would see that the flock got safely to market! Hadn't he done it a hundred times already with the shepherd?

"I can't spare any of the other dogs to go with you," said the farmer. "They'll be busy up here with me to-day. You can manage all right if you keep both your eyes open."

Shadow ran round the little flock of sheep to warn them to bunch together. Then he headed them down the hill to the farm. Johnny was to wait for them there.

Johnny was in a great state of excitement. He felt very grown-up indeed to be taking a flock to market all by himself. That was fine! He yelled to Shadow as soon as he saw him coming with the sheep.

"Hurry up, Shadow! It's ten-past nine! We'll never be in time to meet Uncle Harry at one o'clock! Do hurry!"

If Shadow had been able to laugh out loud, he certainly would have done so. It was fun to see Johnny so excited and important. "Woof!" he said to the sheep. "Keep together, will you? Woof!"

The barks were really to tell Johnny that Shadow was just as pleased and excited as the boy, for Shadow could do anything with the sheep without a single bark. Johnny slung his knapsack over his left shoulder. It had his dinner inside, and some biscuits and a bone for Shadow. At twelve o'clock they would both have their dinner in a field or by the wayside. That would be fun.

The little company set off. Johnny walked behind the flock, taking big steps because he felt grown-up. He had a shepherd's crook with him. Shadow ran beside him as much as he could, though he had to go round the flock every now and again to keep them together.

The sheep *would* go to the hedges and nibble the sweet rich grass in the ditch. Shadow had to nose them away and make them flock again. When they came to a corner, and the road split into two different ways, Shadow had to run to the front and lead the sheep down the right road.

"We are getting on nicely, Shadow," said Johnny, looking at his watch. "Only eleven o'clock—and we are more than half-way there.

We shall have plenty of time to sit down for a rest and a meal at twelve o'clock."

When Johnny met the other boys going along the road, he took even longer steps, and whistled in a most important way. The boys looked at him and at the sheep.

"Taking them to market?" they called.

"Yes," Johnny said. "Got to be there by one. Sorry we can't stop. Come on, Shadow."

The boys stared after Johnny and the sheep and he felt pleased and proud. On and on they all went, down the winding lanes, where the hips and haws shone red and crimson in the autumn hedges.

Sometimes there were great sprays of ripe blackberries to be seen, high up on the hedges. Most of the ones low down had been picked by passing children—but they could not reach the high ones.

But Johnny could reach them easily with his crook! He hooked down spray after spray and ate the ripe berries. They were delicious.

"When we stop for our dinner we'll find a place where there are lots of blackberries," said Johnny. "Then I can pick some to eat with my meal."

At twelve o'clock they came to a wayside common, where blackberries grew by the thousand.

"This will be a fine place to stop," said Johnny. "Shadow, take the sheep a little way on to the common. Then come back here for your dinner. The sheep will be all right."

Soon the sheep were pulling at the short grass between the clumps of gorse bushes, and the boy and his dog were sitting comfortably on tufts of heather, eating a fine meal. Johnny had ham sandwiches with plenty of mustard on them, two slices of home-made ginger cake, and a large piece of bread with a lump of cheese. So he had a very good dinner.

Shadow had his biscuits, and then began to gnaw the bone. He kept his eyes on the sheep in case they wandered too far, and once he jumped up and went after a sheep that had gone quite a long way away.

"Oh, Shadow—do stay here with me and don't keep running away," said Johnny, pulling the sheep-dog down beside him. "You know quite well that the sheep will be all right. Don't fuss!"

After they had finished their meal Johnny went

to pick blackberries. Shadow went with him, wishing that he liked the juicy fruit as much as Johnny did. Johnny gave him two or three of the ripest, but Shadow spat them out. They tasted horrible to him.

Then the dog began to get worried. Time was getting on. They would be late for market! Shadow had no watch, no clock, to guide him—but he had a good sense of time, and he had been to market many times. He knew that they must be there by one o'clock. He barked to Johnny and licked the boy's hand.

"All right, Shadow, all right," said Johnny. "I know it's time we went! I'm just coming. Let me pick this lovely lot of blackberries first—they're the best I've seen!"

At last the boy was ready to start. He looked at his watch. "Good gracious! It's twenty to one! We'll never be in time to meet Uncle Harry! Quick, Shadow, get the sheep! Hurry now, hurry!"

Shadow sped off. He rounded up the flock and led them to Johnny to count. But Johnny did not bother. He was in too great a hurry. He ran his eyes over the sheep.

"Yes—they're all right. Now do come on, Shadow. We'll never be there!"

Shadow felt there was something wrong. He could not count as Johnny could, but he felt that the flock was not quite so big as it was before. Shadow was right. There was a lamb missing. The dog ran round and round the flock, sniffing hard. Johnny shouted to him.

"Shadow! What are you fussing about! Let the sheep go on, for goodness' sake!"

So Shadow headed the sheep on their way, but all the time he felt uncomfortable. He had to depend on Johnny to count the sheep, and he felt certain that the boy would do his duty—and yet there certainly was something wrong about the flock. Shadow suddenly felt as if he must go back to the common and hunt about there. He turned to go.

Johnny yelled to him. "Shadow! Are you mad! *This* is the way we're going, not that!"

They got to the market at ten minutes past one. Uncle Harry was there, waiting. He grinned when he saw Johnny coming with the sheep.

"Hallo, hallo!" he said. "Here we come with our flock, looking most grown-up and important.

Well done, Johnny. I'll take the sheep now and sell them. Go and see if you can buy yourself an ice-cream somewhere or a lemonade drink. You deserve it."

Johnny ran his eye over the sheep. They were all there—but what about the lambs? His heart sank down into his boots—for there were only three, instead of four! Goodness, one had run away and got lost!

Johnny went red. He knew he should tell his uncle. But he would get scolded, and nobody would ever trust him again. He looked at Shadow miserably. The dog knew at once that something was wrong—and he knew what was wrong too! One of the flock was missing! He tugged at Johnny's sleeve.

"Woof!" he said. "Come with me. We'll go and find that sheep! Cheer up, Johnny!"

CHAPTER NINETEEN

SHADOW PUTS THINGS RIGHT

JOHNNY LOOKED down miserably at Shadow. He felt suddenly small and foolish. Why hadn't he kept counting his flock to make quite, quite sure that they were all there? Now, in a short while, his uncle would find out that one was missing, and then he would be very angry with Johnny.

The boy knew that Shadow wanted to go and

find the missing lamb. He patted the dog's head. "We'll go together," he said. "Maybe we'll find it where we had our dinner, Shadow. I should have counted the flock when you rounded them up then. You brought them to me and I didn't count them. I remember that you felt there was something wrong, and I didn't take any notice of you. How silly I've been!"

He turned to go with Shadow—but his uncle suddenly called to him.

"Hie, Johnny! Don't go and get an ice-cream just yet! I've got to go and see about some pigs. Take over the sheep for me for a little while, will you? Put them into that pen over there. I'll be back in a few minutes."

So Johnny couldn't go with Shadow. He hurried over to the sheep, looking white and anxious—but his uncle had walked away to talk to another farmer about pigs, so he did not notice anything.

Johnny herded the sheep into the small pen. They stood there patiently, rubbing their grey, woolly bodies against each other. The market was full of the lowing of cows, the bleating of sheep, the grunting of pigs, and the clucking of hens. Usually Johnny loved it all—but he was too miserable and ashamed to enjoy anything just then.

He would have to tell his uncle about the lost lamb. He turned to speak to Shadow—but the dog was gone. He was nowhere to be seen.

"Shadow! Shadow!" called Johnny. But Shadow did not hear. He had gone to find the lost lamb. The dog had felt certain that all was not right with the flock, although he had not been able to count them. When he knew that one was missing, he had gone round the flock, his keen nose sniffing at each animal. He knew then that one of the lambs was not there.

He heard Johnny's uncle call to him and saw the boy putting the flock into the pen. He guessed he would have to stay there until his uncle came back.

"Then I must go by myself and try to find that sheep," thought Shadow. So he slipped off through the crowd at the market, past the pigs, past the patient cows, and past the hens and the ducks clucking and quacking in their own pens.

The dog ran back down the main road that

led to the market. He did not think that the lamb was anywhere there, for the dog felt certain the lamb had run away whilst he and Johnny had sat down to have their dinner. But all the same he kept his eyes and ears open in case the lamb had trotted after the flock to the market.

But there was no lamb to be seen. The dog soon came to the wayside common where he and Johnny had rested. He began to nose about round all the gorse bushes, sniffing for a fresh smell of sheep.

He smelt the smell of the flock. But he was looking for a newer smell, that would tell him that the lamb had stayed there and was about somewhere.

Round and round the bushes went the dog, sniffing busily. He could not find any fresh smell at all. At last he came to the smell of a lamb that had wandered a good way away. Was it one of the lambs he had got back to the flock—or might it be the runaway lamb?

Shadow sniffed everywhere—and then he found a smell that led right away from the common. The lamb must have wandered a long way—this must be the right trail!

The dog followed it—and then the trail led back to the road again. Here it became mixed with the smell of many sheep. Shadow saw the pattern their little hooves had made on the roadway. He was puzzled.

"These are not our sheep," he thought. "They have a different smell. And yet the lamb went to them. I can smell his smell here and there in the big sheep-smell."

The dog was really puzzled. The sheep flock that the lamb had joined had gone the opposite way—away from the market, not *to* it. Could the lamb have mistaken the flock for its own and gone with it?

Shadow made up his mind to follow it and see. So down the road he ran, sniffing the smell of the flock, and then down a lane, round a corner and down another lane. Then through a gate and into a field.

And there was the flock of sheep he had been following, quietly grazing together. And there, in a corner by itself, lonely and miserable, was the lost lamb! Just as Shadow had thought, it had wandered over the common, quite lost, and then had seen a flock of strange sheep going by. Thinking they were its own flock, the lamb had run up and joined them.

It had gone along with them, not knowing what else to do—and now it was in a strange place, with strange sheep, and was frightened and puzzled.

Shadow ran up to it. He smelt its familiar, well-known smell. The dog knew the smell of every lamb and sheep on the farm. He ran round the lamb in delight.

"I've found you!" he thought. "Now I must get you back to Johnny. I hope the shepherd here won't see me. He may try to stop me! I wonder where the sheep-dogs are, here. They may stop me, too."

At that moment two collie-dogs appeared. They ran barking up to Shadow. He whined to them. They stopped when they saw his tail wagging slightly. They smelt the smell of the lamb nearby, and the smell was strange to them. Then they knew that it was not their lamb, and both the dogs guessed at once that Shadow had come to fetch it.

So they did not try to stop him, but ran with him and the lamb as he took it out of the field.

Shadow was glad. He did not want to fight two dogs!

He guided the lamb down the lane and then to the main road. He made it go quickly. He wanted to get back to Johnny as soon as ever he could. That little lamb had never gone so fast in all its life! It could not think why Shadow made it trot in such a hurry.

But Shadow knew that Johnny would be anxiously waiting for him. Johnny would have guessed that the dog had gone to find the missing lamb.

Johnny did guess, of course. He stood by the pen where he had put the sheep, looking round for Shadow, and wondering when his uncle would come. He could see him far away at the opposite corner of the market, talking earnestly to another farmer. The pigs were close by. Uncle Harry prodded one or two of them with his stick. He was thinking of buying them.

"Oh, I hope he is ages and ages buying them," thought poor Johnny. "I'll simply *have* to tell him that a lamb is missing when he comes over. I must be brave and own up. But how I wish that Shadow would turn up and bring the missing lamb—but there isn't really much hope! I expect the lamb is quite, quite lost."

Uncle Harry finished his talk with the farmer. "I'll come across and see you in half an hour," he said. "And if you'll agree to my price, I'll have the pigs. But I must go over to Johnny, my young nephew, now—the boy has been waiting with the sheep for ages."

Johnny saw his uncle coming over to him and his heart sank. But in a second it beat fast, for what did he see but Shadow coming in at the market entrance with the lamb running in front of him! Johnny could hardly believe his eyes. It *was* the lamb. No doubt about that at all! Good old Shadow—how wonderful he was!

Just as Uncle Harry came up, Shadow pushed the lamb against Johnny's knees. The boy opened the pen and the lamb rushed in, glad to find itself among friends again. It bleated happily.

"Hallo!" said Uncle Harry in surprise. "Did a lamb get out? Are they all there, Johnny? Your father said he was sending sixteen sheep and four lambs. I didn't count them when you brought them. Let me see—one, two, three, four lambs—and one, two, three . . ."

He counted the flock and found that they were all there. He wondered why Johnny had such a red face and said so little, but he thought the boy must be tired.

"Well, thanks for your good work, Johnny," he said. "Sorry to have kept you waiting so long. Tell your father you're a good boy—and go and get yourself your ice-cream!"

He gave Johnny a smile, and the boy smiled back and went off. But he didn't feel that he deserved an ice-cream. He hadn't really been such a good boy as his uncle thought him. He had been careless. If it hadn't been for Shadow he would have got into serious trouble.

The boy and the dog walked back solemnly together. Shadow felt ashamed too. It was not a good thing to let a lamb escape when he was in charge of a flock. Shadow wondered if Johnny would tell anyone about it.

Johnny was wondering about that too. "If I don't say a word, no one will ever know," he thought. "And Dad will trust me again, and think I am clever. Well—I'll see."

He got home at last, tired and hungry. His father met him in the yard. "Hallo, son!" he said.

"Everything all right? Did you hand over the sheep to your uncle?"

"Yes, Dad," said Johnny, going red.

"I guess Uncle Harry was pleased with you, wasn't he?" said the farmer, putting his arm round Johnny's shoulder.

"Yes, Dad," said Johnny.

"Well, so am I!" said the farmer. "You're a good lad. It's not many boys of your age could be trusted to take a flock to market and get there safe and sound. Well done!"

But that was too much for Johnny. He was an honest boy, and he could not bear to be praised when he knew he had been careless.

"Don't say that, Dad," he said. "I got to market with one lamb missing—all my own fault, because I didn't count them after I'd had my dinner—and if it hadn't been for old Shadow here, who went back and found the lamb somehow, we'd have been one lamb short, and it couldn't have been sold. I'm sorry about it, Dad. I know you'll never trust me again—but I had to tell you."

"Of course, you had!" said his father, patting him on the shoulder. "Why shouldn't you tell me? And why shouldn't I trust you again? Why, I shall trust you all the more, now that I know you're such an honest little fellow! I'm proud of you! You wouldn't take the praise I gave you, because you didn't deserve it—and you owned up like a brave boy. Cheer up—and here's a shilling to buy yourself something, for taking my flock to market."

"Oh, thanks, Dad," said Johnny, his face shining at his father's words. "You're fine, Dad. It's not many boys that have got a father like *you*. Thanks for not scolding me. I'll *never* be careless again."

"I know that," said the farmer, and went off to feed the pigs, glad to have such a brave and honest little son.

"Shadow, I'm not spending this shilling on myself," said Johnny. "I'm spending it on you! You're the one that found the lamb. Come on—you're going to have a shilling's-worth of the butcher's best meat!"

You should have heard Shadow bark! He loved the meat—and how he loved Johnny for thinking of such a treat!

CHAPTER TWENTY

THE THIEVES IN THE FARMYARD

JOHNNY'S MOTHER was very proud of her hens. She and Johnny counted the eggs each day, put so many aside for use at home, and sold the rest.

"You know, Johnny, my hens make quite a nice bit of money for me," said his mother. "They are laying very well, and the year-old hens are doing better than ever. I do feel pleased."

"I'm pleased too," said Johnny. "You'll be able to sell some of the hens too, Mother—and the young ducklings will bring you some money as well."

The farmyard was always a gay place in the springtime, with young chicks and ducklings around, and plenty of calves, lambs, and foals. Johnny loved to walk through the big farmyard and hear all the many noises—the clucks and cheeps, the quacks and cackles, the moos and bleats. It all sounded so young and fresh and alive.

"I wouldn't be happy living anywhere except on a farm," said Johnny to Shadow. "What do you think about it, old chap?"

Shadow thought exactly the same, and said so with a big wag of his tail. He licked Johnny's hand.

"I love living on a farm with you, Johnny," the lick said, "but I'd be happy anywhere so long as I was with you, my little master!"

"Shadow, haven't we a lot of ducklings and chicks this spring!" said Johnny happily. "Mother will be so pleased to see them doing well. She has promised me a watch if she makes enough money.

I've never had a watch of my own. Shadow, wouldn't it be fine?"

Shadow wanted Johnny to have a watch. The old shepherd had one—a great big old thing that ticked almost as loudly as a clock. All the dogs knew it. It told the shepherd when it was their dinner-time, and so they all liked to see him taking his enormous watch out of his pocket. The shepherd usually went more by the sun than by his watch—but he grumbled about the new summer-time, and said it put him right out of his reckoning!

The young ducklings were in charge of three hens. Johnny's mother had set clutches of ducks' eggs under the hens, and every egg but one had hatched.

"Why don't you let the ducks hatch out their own eggs, Mother?" asked Johnny.

"They are not very good mothers," said his mother. "They leave their eggs rather too long and let them get cold. Then they don't hatch. Or they get tired of sitting after a while, and desert them. But hens are good mothers and don't mind how long they sit."

Five hens had hatched out clutches of hens' eggs

and had brought off fifty-two chicks—so the farmyard was very full indeed! The tiny birds ran everywhere—and, dear me, what an excitement when the ducklings saw the pond for the first time!

They ran straight to it, and paddled in the edge of the water, cheeping loudly. The mother-hen ran after them, squawking at the top of her voice. Johnny was in the dairy, helping his mother to count eggs, when they heard the noise.

"Johnny, quick—go and see what's happening!" said his mother. "It sounds as if one of the hens is hurt."

Johnny rushed out, with Shadow at his heels—and when he saw what the matter was, how he laughed! His mother heard him laughing and came out.

"Oh!" she said, "that's always a funny sight to see! The hens get so upset when they see the ducklings going into the water for the first time. You see, they don't seem to know that their young ones are ducklings, not chicks, and so they fear the water for them. My goodness, what a scolding those ducklings will get when they come out!"

The ducklings took not a bit of notice of their

hen-mother. They splashed with glee in the pond—and then one duckling, bolder than the rest, pushed himself right out of his depth, and swam off, cheeping loudly.

"Eee, eee, eee, look at me! Eee, eee, eee, look at me!" At least, that is what Johnny said it was saying. The other ducklings stared at him, and then followed him with little squeaks of excitement. One by one they sailed off on the pond, absurd little mites of yellow and black, their tiny tails wagging in glee. The big ducks looked at them in surprise.

The poor mother-hen put one foot into the water herself, half meaning to go after her disobedient brood. But the water felt cold and wet and she took her foot out again in a hurry.

"Cluck, cluck!" she said in horror. "Come out, you bad children! This water is wet and cold. Wait till it is warm and dry."

"Eee, eee, eee, we've gone to sea!" cheeped the ducklings—or so Johnny said. His mother laughed at him.

"What funny things you say, Johnny!" she said. "You make me laugh."

"I suppose we *can* count our chickens and

ducklings now they are hatched," said Johnny. "Oh, Mother, what fun when they are all well grown and you can sell them! You will really get a lot of money!"

"And you shall have your watch," said his mother, going back into the dairy. "Then, dear me, you will have no excuse at all for being late for meals."

Johnny counted the chicks and the ducklings. It was difficult because they moved about so. There were a great many. Johnny thought he had never seen such a lot in his farmyard before.

But he had counted them too soon—for the next day, alas, seven of the little yellow-and-black ducklings were missing! Johnny counted them again and again—but it was no good, he couldn't get to the right number. Seven were quite plainly gone. He went to tell his mother.

"Oh, dear!" she said. "I wonder if the rats have dared to come into the yard again. They did a lot of damage to my young birds the year before last. Since old Tibby-Cat has died, perhaps they have dared to come into the yard again. She was such a wonderful ratter."

"Mother, it's dreadful to lose seven young

ducklings all at once," said Johnny. "I shall tell Shadow. Perhaps he can find out what is happening for me."

"Shadow is busy all day long with the new lambs and the sheep," said his mother. "The shepherd can't spare him for a while, Johnny."

"But he sleeps with me at night," said Johnny. "If I tell him about the missing ducklings, perhaps he could keep a watch at night."

"He is tired out at night," said his mother. "Never mind, Johnny—I always expect to lose a few of the young birds, and after all, we had far more hatched out than we expected."

But all the same Johnny did tell Shadow. The sheep-dog listened with his head on one side and his large brown eyes wide open.

"Shadow, I think the rats are stealing our ducklings," said Johnny. "Look out for me, will you? I won't have my watch if we lose many more, you know—and besides, it is horrid to think of those dear little ducklings being caught by the fierce cruel rats."

Shadow was always tired after his long day up on the hills. He had to run for miles, herding the sheep, guarding them, taking flocks to new pastures, and keeping the young lambs with their mothers. The spring-time was always a busy time for the sheep-dogs. They did nearly all the work for the shepherd.

But although the dog was tired and sleepy at night, and longed to curl up on Johnny's toes and go sound asleep, he did not once think of doing so if there were rats to be dealt with! Now that old Tibby-Cat had died, the rats were bolder. Shadow knew it. He had smelt their tracks all around the yard. He went to speak to Jessie, the yard-dog, about it.

Jessie was Shadow's mother, a lovely collie-dog. But she was old now, and could not smell so sharply, nor hear so well as she once did. Shadow asked her about the rats.

"Yes," she said. "They are about again. I am not quick enough now to go ratting—but you, Shadow, should be able to catch and nip them well. Come out here to-night and we will watch for them!"

So Shadow, sleepy and tired though he was, lay down quietly beside his mother's kennel, watching and waiting. And it was not long before he heard the pattering of tiny feet and the high squeaks of the rats who were coming to steal the young ducklings for their supper.

Shadow was out among them in a trice. He was surprisingly quick, and pounced on this rat and that one just as if he were a fox-terrier. He nipped each rat sharply at the back of the neck and killed it. The rats fled away with squeaks of terror.

"They won't come again," said Shadow, pleased. "Our chicks and ducklings are safe enough now. Seven rats—Johnny will be pleased!"

Shadow wondered whether to take the rats to show Johnny in bed—but he thought that Johnny's mother would not like that. She did not even like bones taken to Johnny's room—and she would certainly make a fuss if she saw seven rats on the bed.

How pleased Johnny was the next morning! "Good old Shadow!" he said. "I knew you would help us. You always do. Now we shall be all right, and all our hens and ducks will be safe!"

But Johnny was wrong! Another enemy came to the farmyard—a much bigger one than the rats. In one night three hens were killed and taken away! Who could the enemy be?

CHAPTER TWENTY-ONE

A VERY CUNNING ENEMY

WHEN JOHNNY found that three hens were gone, he stared in horror. He had gone to the hen-house to open it and let out the hens early that morning. He did not usually count them, because he thought they were quite safe in the big hen-house.

But just outside the hen-house he saw a lot of feathers on the ground. He looked at them. They were red hen-feathers—feathers from one or more of his mother's pretty red-brown hens!

Johnny looked quickly at the hens. They seemed rather frightened that morning, and bunched together as if they wanted to protect one another. Johnny could count them easily.

"*Three* missing!" he said aloud, in dismay. "Gracious! I hoped there would be only one gone—but there are three. Mother! Come quickly!"

His mother came running out, wondering what the matter was. "Look!" said Johnny. "Some enemy came in the night and killed and took away three of our hens. Who could it be? A gypsy, do you think?"

"No," said his mother. "A gypsy would never leave tell-tale feathers like that. No—it's a fox!"

"A fox!" said Johnny. "I never thought of that. But, Mother—could a fox carry *three* hens away?"

"He would come back each time and take away one," said his mother. "No doubt it is a fox that has a family of cubs. They are very fond of poultry. Oh, Johnny—how tiresome this is! Once a fox has been able to kill hens at a farm, he keeps coming back. We must find out where he got in."

The two of them, and Shadow, went round the hen-house. It was Shadow who found out where the fox got into the house. He smelt the strong fox-smell all around, of course, but it was very strong indeed where the fox had squeezed himself in between two half-broken boards at the back of the house. There were more feathers there too.

"That's where he got in," said Johnny. "I'll mend that to-day, Mother."

So he mended up the hole, and put two new boards in the place of the old ones. Shadow sat and watched him.

"That's to stop the cunning old fox from getting in!" Johnny told Shadow. "Fancy, Shadow—poor Mother has lost all those ducklings and now three hens! Isn't it just too bad?"

Thump-thump went Shadow's tail on the ground. He hoped that nothing more would happen to Johnny's mother's hens and ducks. He knew that foxes were very cunning creatures indeed. He licked Johnny's hand and bounded off to the hills. He had heard the shepherd whistling to him.

He spoke to Rafe and Dandy about the fox. They knew all about him.

"He's an old fellow, very sharp and cunning," said Tinker. "He's lived on that hill over there for years. He's been hunted time and again but he's never been caught. He has a wife and a family of cubs now—that's why he has begun to thieve from the farmyard. He'll be at it again—so keep your eyes open, Shadow. We've never been able to catch him—but maybe you'll be luckier."

When Johnny went to open the hen-house the next morning, he had a great shock again. In the hen-run, just outside the hen-house, were many hen-feathers blowing about in the wind! Surely, surely, it couldn't mean that the fox had been again?

But that was exactly what those feathers did mean! When Johnny counted his hens he found that there were two more missing.

"Mother! How *could* the fox have got into the hen-house this time?" said the boy, really puzzled. "I mended that hole. I've been all round the hen-house and there isn't another hole anywhere for the fox to get in."

"He jumped over the wire netting of the hen-run," said his father, looking up at the wire that ran six feet high around the run. "Foxes jump well. That's what he did."

"But, Dad, how could he get into the house to get the hens?" asked Johnny.

His father looked at the hen-house. It had sliding windows at the front. One of them was opened at the top to let in a little air. He pointed to it.

"He got in through that crack," he said. "A fox can make himself very slender when he likes—and that's how he got in last night. Jumped up to the window, landed on the top, squeezed in through the narrow opening—and took the hens! I heard old Jessie barking last night—if I'd thought it was a fox she was barking at I'd have come out."

"Oh, Dad, I do hope he won't come again," said Johnny. "Shadow! Can't you catch that cunning old fox?"

Shadow licked Johnny's leg. He too had heard Jessie barking the night before, and he had half got up to go and see what the matter was. But he had had a hard day on the hills and was tired out—and he had fallen asleep again before he had made up his mind what to do. And now two more hens had gone! That was bad luck.

That night Shadow, tired as he was, would not sleep on Johnny's bed. He meant to watch for the fox. He lay down in the deep shadow beside Jessie's kennel, watching for the fox to come in the moonlight. But he didn't come.

For four nights Shadow kept watch and the fox did not come. On the fifth night Johnny spoke to him.

"Come and sleep on my bed to-night, Shadow, old fellow. I have missed you dreadfully these last nights. I don't think the fox will come again."

Shadow wanted to watch for the fox again, but Johnny so badly longed for Shadow on his bed that the dog gave in. And that night he lay on the boy's feet as usual. But he could not sleep. He felt sure that there was trouble in the farmyard that night—and when he heard Jessie beginning to bark he was sure of it. He leapt off the bed and went to the door. It was shut!

Shadow ran to the window. That was open—

but it was a high jump to the ground. Another bark from Jessie decided him. He jumped right out of the window to the ground below! Luckily he fell on a flower-bed, and rolled over. He was up in a trice and ran to the farmyard. He spoke to Jessie, the farmyard dog.

"No—there's no one in the hen-house," said Jessie. "But hark how the ducks are quacking down by the pond. That's what made me bark!"

Shadow sped down to the pond. The ducks were quacking in fright. Shadow saw them bunched together on one of the banks of the pond. They had been swimming in the moonlight.

On the other side of the pond was a shadow moving in the shelter of a hedge. Shadow's sharp eyes saw it. He also saw a splash of white moving with the shadow, and the dog knew at once what it was.

"It's the fox, carrying off a white duck!" thought Shadow. "I'm after him!"

Shadow raced round the other side of the pond. The fox had already seen the dog and was running fast over the field. He slipped through a gap in the hedge. He was still carrying the duck.

Shadow tore after him. His nose told him the

way the fox had gone, as well as his eyes. He meant to catch that cunning old fox, if he had to run all night!

The fox dropped the duck. He could not run fast enough, carrying a heavy bird. The duck waddled off, squawking. It was not much hurt. Shadow wondered if it would have the sense to go back to its pond.

On and on flew the fox and the dog. The fox played all the tricks he knew to break his scent so that Shadow could not follow him. He jumped a stream, wading up a little way—and instead of going out on the opposite bank, he jumped out on to the same side, but a little way farther up. But Shadow knew the tricks of foxes. Rafe had often told him about them.

So instead of going into the moonlit water the dog ran along the bank, keeping his eyes on the dark head of the swimming fox. He was after him at once when he came out of the stream again.

Once the fox jumped up on a wall, when he was for a minute out of sight of Shadow. He crouched there, hoping that the dog would run right by. Then the fox meant to jump down and run the opposite way. Ah, he was a wily old fox!

But Shadow was wily too. As soon as the scent of the fox came to a sudden end below the wall, Shadow guessed at once that the fox was either on top of the wall or had jumped to the other side. And up jumped Shadow too!

The fox got a terrible fright, for the dog jumped almost on top of him! Down he leapt, just in time, and the two of them raced for miles and miles over the hills. They both grew tired.

Then the fox came to an old hole of his, six or seven miles away from the farm. He ran down it, panting and exhausted, his tongue hanging out. Shadow came to a stop at the entrance to the den. A strong smell of fox came up.

"I can't get down!" thought Shadow. "I'm too big! This last trick of the fox is too good for me!"

The fox barked deep down in his den.

"Go away! I shall stay here for days if I like! You will never get me. But you are the swiftest dog I have ever run against. I shall not come near your farm again. I will not have my young ones chased by dogs like you. I shall go to fetch my mate and my cubs and bring them here. We shall never come near you again."

"Do you mean that?" barked Shadow. "If you do, I will leave you alone. I know it is your nature to hunt birds and young animals—and I do not blame you for that. But if you come to rob Johnny's farm, then I shall hunt you and kill you and all your family! Do you hear, Red Fox?"

The fox heard. He said no more. Shadow left the hole and went back to the farm, tired out but happy. He felt quite certain that never again would the fox rob Johnny's farmyard. Johnny would get his watch. Shadow was happy.

He jumped in through a downstairs window and padded up to Johnny's room. He scratched on the door. Johnny awoke and opened it.

"Wherever have you been, Shadow?" said Johnny sleepily, as the dog curled up on his feet once more, panting and tired. "Hunting foxes? Clever dog, aren't you!"

Ah, Johnny, Shadow had been cleverer than you guessed, that night!

CHAPTER TWENTY-TWO

BAD DAYS ON THE FARM

SHADOW was three years old when bad days came to the farm. The farmer's corn failed, and he had to plough it into the ground, it was so bad. Then he lost half his sheep with some strange illness, which nearly broke the shepherd's heart.

One of his finest calves died, and then the cows

got into a field where a poisonous weed grew, and two of them sickened and died too.

The farmer looked gloomy as he went about his work. Johnny was sad. His mother worked hard with the hens and ducks, trying to make enough money out of them to pay for the things she needed in the house. The dogs sometimes went short of food, but they did not complain.

The sheep-trials came on again, and this time Shadow defeated even clever Rafe. He won more prizes at the trials than any dog had ever won before, and for once in a way the farmer smiled.

"If that dog could speak, he could teach us a lot," said the farmer to Johnny. "He is a real wonder!"

Somebody else thought that Shadow was wonderful too. An American had been watching the trials, and after they were over, he came to Johnny's father.

"Sir," he said, "I'd like to buy your dog. I own cinemas over in America, and I guess if I made a film of that dog of yours, he'd bring me a fortune. I never saw such a dog in my life. Will you sell him?"

"No, of course not," said Johnny at once. He

was standing nearby. The farmer looked at the American.

"What price would you pay for a dog like that?" he asked.

"Anything you like to name," said the man.

"You must be mad!" said the farmer, and walked off.

"Hie, sir! It's you that are mad, and not me!" shouted the man, hurrying after him. "What would you say if I offered you two hundred and fifty pounds for that dog of yours?"

"I'd still say you were mad," said the farmer. "He's not worth that, and you know it."

"He is, to me," said the American. "Why, two hundred and fifty pounds is nothing! I'll make it three hundred."

Three hundred pounds! Enough to pay off all the losses of the last year, and begin again. Three hundred pounds! That might save the farm, and would be a great help, anyway. The farmer paused and the rich American went on and on talking.

"What's a dog to you? You've plenty! Let me buy him, and you'll see him next year in your cinema show in the next big town. My, I'll do him proud! I'll make him the most famous dog in the world!"

"Well," said the farmer, "well—I don't know. He belongs to Johnny here. We'll have to think about it. Come down to the farm to-morrow and we'll tell you."

The farmer and Johnny walked off. Johnny's heart was heavy and sad. Could his father really mean to sell dear old Shadow? What was the use of having a dog of your own if somebody else had the power to sell him? And yet, could Johnny possibly refuse, when the money meant so much to his father?

That night Johnny, his father, and his mother talked about Shadow and if they should sell him. Shadow sat at the boy's feet, his head on Johnny's knee. He knew what everyone was saying. He could not believe it.

Leave Johnny, the person he loved with all his heart? Why, he couldn't live without Johnny! He was quite sure he couldn't. Never to hear the boy's clear voice again, never to feel Johnny's kind hand on his head! Shadow couldn't bear the thought. He began to whimper.

"Oh, Shadow," said Johnny, with tears in his

eyes, "you know what we're saying, don't you? Oh, Shadow, I can't bear it either—but sometimes, for the sake of the people we love, we have to put up with things we really can't bear. I can't bear to lose you—but I must help my father if I can. I know I must. Oh, Shadow, Shadow—I wish you were not such a clever dog, then no one would have wanted to buy you!"

Then Shadow wished too that he had been a stupid dog. But he had taken such a pride in being clever—now it was his very cleverness that was going to rob him of Johnny. The dog's tail dropped between his legs and his eyes looked mournfully up at Johnny.

Soon it was quite decided. The farmer took hold of Johnny's hand and patted it. He was very sorry for the boy.

"Johnny, I hate to do it. I hate to make you part with Shadow. I love the dog myself. He's quite perfect, and those eyes of his almost speak. Johnny—if you're too sad about it, we won't do it. There's just a chance that the farm will pull through all right without the money."

Johnny shook his head. "I'd rather lose Shadow than have you lose the farm you've been on all your life, Dad," he said. Then he could say no more. He got up and went into the yard, his heart aching, and Shadow followed him closely. He did not mean to lose one minute of Johnny's company, now that he knew he was going across the sea to a big country called America.

He was to go with the American that day week. It was all planned. Shadow told the other dogs and they were sad too, for Shadow was a great favourite of theirs.

"I shan't leave Johnny for a moment now," said Shadow. "Not for one moment!"

But he did, and this is how it came about. He was walking with Johnny in the Long Field, when the boy suddenly gave a loud shout.

"Look! What's that struggling in the ditch over there, Shadow? Is it a cow? Oh, don't say Dad's going to have some more bad luck!"

The two raced to the ditch—and there, sure enough, was a big red-and-white cow. She had tried to reach over to some juicy-looking tufts of grass across the ditch and had fallen in. Now she couldn't get out, for the ditch was deep.

"Shadow! Run down to the farm and get my father," ordered Johnny. So Shadow had to leave

Johnny and race down to the farm. The farmer knew that the dog had come on some errand and he shaded his eyes and looked over the fields. Johnny waved wildly to him.

"Cow in the ditch, I suppose," groaned the farmer. He went to the shed and took down a rope. Then off he went to the Long Field, with Shadow at his heels.

"Do you think she has broken any legs, Dad?" asked Johnny anxiously. "I can't see."

"Oh, I expect she's broken them all!" said the farmer gloomily. "Just my luck!"

The two of them began to drag the cow out with the rope. She came with a rush and the farmer and Johnny sat down with a bump. The cow whisked her tail, walked a few steps, and began to eat the grass.

"Not a single leg broken!" said Johnny. "Hurrah!" The boy was so pleased that he leapt right over the ditch, and Shadow followed him.

And then something horrid happened. Shadow felt something clawing at his eyes and he jerked himself back. It was a strand of rusty barbed wire that the dog had not seen. He blinked his eyes because they were bleeding.

"Dad! Look what Shadow has done!" cried Johnny, kneeling down to look at his dog. "Oh, Dad—will he be blind?"

Poor Shadow was in a very bad way. The wire had torn both his lovely brown eyes, and the dog could not see as he made his way home. He kept close to Johnny's heels and smelt his way instead of seeing.

The boy was beside himself with grief. His father took out the wagon at once and they drove the dog to the doctor. The vet., who knew all about animals, shook his head gravely when he saw the dog.

"I don't know if I can save the sight of both eyes," he said. "One perhaps—but the other is very bad."

He bathed them, put lotion on a pad, and bound up Shadow's head. The dog was puzzled and unhappy. He sat close to Johnny, trying to paw the bandage off his head. But Johnny told him he mustn't touch it.

"Dad! I suppose the American won't want Shadow now, will he?" suddenly said the boy.

"Good gracious! I'd forgotten about that," said the farmer. "No—he won't. A blind dog would be no use at all. I must let him know at once."

"Oh, Dad—I'm sorry about the three hundred pounds, but you simply don't *know* how glad I am to be able to keep Shadow, even if he does go blind," said Johnny, his arms tightly round the big dog. When Shadow heard these words, his heart beat fast in joy. Not to leave Johnny after all? Well, what did his eyes matter then? He was glad, glad, glad that the accident had happened!

"Oh, Shadow, don't jump about like that, you'll loosen the bandage!" cried Johnny, as the dog leapt about in delight, trying to lick the master he could not see.

The American was cross about Shadow. He said he certainly did not want a blind dog, and he blamed Johnny for being careless with him. The boy said nothing at all, but was very glad to think that this rich, bad-tempered man was not going to have anything to do with Shadow.

The strange thing was, that as soon as the American had refused to pay any money for Shadow, things began to go well on the farm. The farmer sold some pigs for the highest prices he had ever known. A field of crops did twice as well as he had expected.

And then, most unexpected of all, a friend to whom the farmer had once lent a hundred pounds, which had never been paid back, sent the money.

"Just look at this!" cried the farmer, waving the cheque in the air. "A hundred pounds out of the blue! I never thought old Harry could possibly pay me back—but he has, bless him! My word, things are looking up!"

Johnny was glad. He would have been gladder, if only dear old Shadow's eyes were all right. He often looked at the dog, sitting so patiently nearby, with his eyes bandaged firmly. The vet. would tell him whether one eye would be saved, when he next took off the bandage.

Johnny took Shadow to the vet. the next day. With gentle hands the doctor took off the bandage. He pressed back the eyelids and looked at the hurt eyes. Then he gave a cry of surprise.

"This is extraordinary! Both eyes are almost healed—even this very bad one! I can't understand it. The dog must be very healthy and strong. Johnny, he won't be blind even in one eye. I believe he'll see as well as ever once they are healed!"

Johnny listened, with tears running down his cheeks. This was the best news of all! Shadow wasn't going to be blind, even in one eye! He would be as perfect as ever. It was too good to be true. He laid his hand on the dog's head, and Shadow tasted the saltiness of Johnny's tears running over his nose. He knew that his master was glad, not sad, and he licked his face lovingly.

He was happy. He was not going to leave Johnny. He was always going to belong to him. And he could see again out of his eyes. That horrid bandage was off!

"Now you must see that he doesn't scratch his eyes at all," said the vet. "He's a marvellous fellow to have got over this so well. Good dog, good dog!"

Johnny made Shadow a large round cardboard collar, which he laced to his leather collar. The dog found that he could not put up his paw to scratch his eyes, because the collar was in the way. The other dogs laughed at him, because of the strange big collar—but Shadow didn't care.

"Johnny makes me wear it because he loves me

enough to want my eyes to get better," he told the other dogs. And in two more weeks the collar was taken off, because Shadow's eyes were quite healed.

"It was good luck for you and me that you hurt your eyes, old fellow!" Johnny said as he took off the cardboard collar. "You never know when bad luck is going to turn out good luck in the end!"

CHAPTER TWENTY-THREE

THE COMING OF THE EAGLE

IN THE early months of the year Johnny loved to go with the sheep to the highest hills around the farm. One of them was so high that on the map it was called Cogill Mountain. Only in the early spring and summer were the sheep taken there, for later on in the year the grass on Cogill was poor, and when the winter came there was always deep snow.

The sheep loved to go to Cogill Mountain. The dogs rounded them up, and then, at a sign from the shepherd—just a whistle or a wave of his arm—they would slowly take the sheep along the rough way to Cogill.

It was such a long way, and so steep in places, that not until Johnny was big and strong would his father allow him to go.

"Keep an eye on Johnny, Andy," the farmer said to the old shepherd. "You know how he always likes to choose the very steepest places, and try to jump the widest streams. Just see he behaves himself. If not, send him home!"

Johnny grinned. He knew quite well that the shepherd would not send him home, no matter what he did. Andy smiled too. He knew how strong and brave Johnny was—there was no fear of him being silly!

Shadow loved going up the mountain. He thought it was fun to take the sheep there, and he decided that the sheep were not quite so silly as he had thought them to be when he saw how sure-footed they were on the narrowest rocky pathway.

Andy, the shepherd, had a rough hut in a sheltered hollow of the mountain near the top. It was built of wood, and Andy used to stuff the cracks and holes with heather to make them rain-tight and wind-tight. Johnny helped him.

"I'm going to stay the night with you, Andy," he said. "For the first time! Dad said I might, didn't he? Oh, it *will* be fun to sleep up here on the mountain! Shadow will think it's funny to lie on a bed of heather instead of my blanket at home!"

Shadow did think it was funny, but he liked the smell of heather very much. He watched with great interest as the shepherd and Johnny tore up armfuls of heather and took them to the hut.

First the cracks were stuffed up. Then beds of heather were put down in one corner, with a rug or two thrown over them.

The shepherd and Johnny had brought their own food with them. They put it high on a nail, hung in a stout bag. Andy knew what hungry dogs would do to a good meal if they could get at it.

Johnny was tired after his long walk from the farm to the top of the mountain. He went to the door of the hut and sat down just outside. It was about half-past twelve and the sun was high. Below Johnny lay the peaceful mountain-side, dotted with white sheep. Most of the lambs of that year were big now and strong, quite able to journey to the mountain with their mothers.

Andy came to stand beside Johnny. He pointed to where a lamb was standing by itself, not frisking with the others. "That lamb's a weakling," he said. "It doesn't grow as it should. And there's another one over there, Johnny. Maybe this good mountain air and growing grass will make them as bonny as the others."

Shadow lay down at Johnny's feet. He too knew the weakling lambs, for they had been difficult to take up the mountain. Too often they had stopped and bleated pitifully. Their mothers waited for them at first, but after a while they became tired of the bleating lambs and took no notice. Then the dogs had to send on the lambs, and Shadow got very cross with one youngster because it would keep running the wrong way.

But the dog knew enough to be patient. He

might *feel* cross, but it was no good showing it. Hot temper and anger were of no use in dealing with sheep. It only made them more frightened than ever!

Johnny had once told Shadow that anyone could tell what the master of the farm was like by noticing the way that his dogs rounded up the sheep.

"If the dogs are snappy and impatient with the sheep, you may be sure that the farmer is a bad-tempered man," said Johnny. "But if the dogs are patient and quiet, it is quite certain that their master is the same!"

That made Shadow quite determined to be patient with the sheep, for he did not want anyone to think that Johnny was anything but good and patient too. So although the silly lamb made him feel very angry, the dog did not show it once, and very soon the little creature sensed that the strong, quiet animal behind it, nosing it upwards, was its friend, and not its enemy. Then it went more willingly and did not stop so often.

Johnny and the shepherd had their meal out on the sunny mountain-side. The five dogs lay around them, waiting for any scraps. Each dog was fairly treated, and all had their turn. They knew this and did not fight. They watched the sheep as they lay, keeping a wary eye for any that might start to wander back down the hill. Once the sheep had settled in they would be quite all right, but there were always one or two who had the idea that they would like to wander back home.

As the shepherd, the boy, and the dogs sat or lay peacefully there, gazing down the still mountain-side, the shepherd lifted his eyes to the sky. Something had caught his attention there. He narrowed his bright blue eyes and looked hard at what he saw.

"What is it, Andy?" asked Johnny, looking up too. The boy saw a big black speck soaring round and round in the sky, going higher and higher on outspread wings.

"Do you know what that is?" said Andy. "It's an eagle!"

"An eagle!" said Johnny in surprise. "I don't think I've ever seen one before, Andy. It must be a very big bird."

"It's enormous," said Andy. "Ten years ago eagles nested on the other side of this mountain, and I had to watch my sheep and lambs from dawn till dusk!"

"Why? Surely birds don't hurt sheep!" said Johnny in surprise.

"Eagles do, if they are daring enough," said the shepherd. "They will swoop down on weakly lambs and carry them off to their nest for their young ones to feast on!"

"Goodness!" said Johnny, amazed. "I shouldn't have thought that any bird was strong enough to do that. Oh, Andy—you don't think the eagles will come after *our* sheep, do you?"

"No—I shouldn't think so," said the shepherd, still staring at the black speck soaring in the sky. "Although eagles are strong, powerful birds, they are rather cowardly when it comes to attacking anything bigger than themselves. A hare, a rabbit, a sickly lamb—they will drop on those without fear—but if a mother-sheep runs at them they will fly off at once."

Johnny stood watching the soaring bird. It came down lower on its outspread wings. They were really enormous wings, and the tips turned upwards, the feathers spread out like fingers against the sky. Now and again the bird flapped its wings slowly and majestically as it soared and glided.

"I wish I could do that!" said Johnny. "Fly up high in the sky like that, and then glide on the wind for ages! When I'm grown up I shall fly an aeroplane."

The eagle at last flew down low and disappeared behind the other side of the mountain. Johnny was all eagerness to go and see where it had gone.

"All right," said the shepherd, "but don't lose yourself or fall down a cliff or anything like that! Take Shadow and Dandy with you."

The two dogs ran joyfully off with the boy. It was fun to climb right to the rocky top of the mountain on that clear spring afternoon. When Johnny got to the top, he looked down on the other side. It was steep and rocky. He wondered where the eagle had its nest.

Then he saw the great bird standing nobly and majestically on a high rock, some way down the mountain-side. It looked magnificent, most powerful and fierce. Its great hooked beak and piercing eyes seemed cruel to Johnny. He wondered whether or not he dared to go any nearer. But how he would love to see its nest!

The eagle had not seen him. It suddenly gave a curious yelping scream, and rose slowly into the air, its huge wings making it seem three times as large at once. And then, from somewhere below, another eagle rose into the sky.

"They must have a nest nearby!" thought the boy in excitement. "Down Shadow! Down, Dandy! Keep quiet!"

The dogs lay quietly, though the fur along their necks had risen up at the sight of the great birds. Johnny waited until they had soared over the mountain-top and then he made his way to where the first eagle had been standing so majestically. It was a steep and rocky climb—and Johnny found that he could not reach the nest itself, for it was built on a ledge of the cliff-side so rocky and steep that it was impossible to get near it without a rope.

But he could see the nest easily. It was made of branches and twigs, with heather as well, and was built up to quite a height. The cup of the nest was lined with moss, grass, and heather tufts, and with something soft that looked like rushes.

In the nest were two young eagles. They lay quietly there, and made no movement. Johnny watched them for a while and then made his way back up the mountain, excited to think that he had found an eagle's nest. The great eagles themselves soared above him. They were dark-brown, and had some golden feathers gleaming on their necks at the back. The dogs growled as the birds came lower.

"Be quiet, Shadow," ordered Johnny. "The eagles are doing no harm!"

But Johnny could not say that when the next morning dawned. He and the shepherd slept the night in the old hut, cosy and warm on their bed of heather, and were up as soon as the sun rose in the eastern sky.

Johnny awoke first, aroused by the growling of the dogs, and then by the loud barking of Shadow, excited and anxious.

What a stange sight met his eyes! One of the eagles, its enormous wings outspread, was carrying off in its fierce talons the smallest of the sickly lambs! It was a heavy weight to carry, but the eagle was very powerful, and its strong wings took it slowly up the mountain and over the top to its nest.

"Andy! The eagle! It's taken one of those two

lambs!" shouted Johnny, quite beside himself with worry, for he could not possibly do anything to save the lamb. The eagle gave a curious yelp and disappeared over the brow of the mountain. The dogs barked madly.

The shepherd was angry and yet helpless to do anything. Dogs were of no use against eagles. Only a gun would help.

"Johnny, I'll have to leave you in charge of the sheep this morning; whilst I go to fetch my gun," said Andy. "I'll be back as soon as possible. If the eagle comes again, shout at it and wave your arms. Keep the dogs close by you."

Andy strode off quickly down the mountain. He did not think that the eagle would come again whilst he was gone. But he was wrong!

CHAPTER TWENTY-FOUR

A MOUNTAIN ADVENTURE

JOHNNY KEPT a sharp watch for the eagle, but for a long time he did not even see the soaring speck in the sky that told where the enormous bird was taking its wonderful flight. He felt hungry, so he busied himself getting some breakfast. The dogs kept one eye on him and one on the sheep. They were hungry too.

Johnny made himself some cheese sandwiches and boiled a tin kettle over a fire he made. He was soon munching his sandwiches and drinking hot tea, and thinking that never had food tasted so nice before!

The dogs were uneasy. They had not seen an eagle robbing a flock before, and it puzzled them and upset them.

Shadow especially was worried. He had seen the bird's enormous claws or talons, and he did not see why the bird should not attack him and Dandy and Johnny, as much as any of the sheep.

"Don't worry, Shadow," said Dandy. "You heard the shepherd say that eagles are not usually brave enough to attack even a grown sheep who defends her lambs—so how could they possibly dare to attack us or Johnny?"

"I don't know," said Shadow uneasily. "I smell danger, Dandy. You see to the sheep this morning. I want to keep close to Johnny."

"Oh, no! You come and do your share of the work!" said Dandy at once. "I can see where some of the sheep have wandered too far, and I am not going to fetch them back alone. You must come and help me. We can do the work in half the time if there are two of us on the job."

So Shadow had to go with Dandy. He always obeyed the older dogs, for he knew they had taught him everything and he owed them a great deal. So he got up and followed Dandy when Johnny shouted to the older dog that he wanted the sheep fetched in closer.

"Don't let any of them wander too far," said Johnny, giving Shadow a passing pat. "I'd like to have them all under my eye with these eagles about, Shadow."

So the two dogs had a good morning's work to do. They rounded up the wandering sheep, and sent back all the naughty little lambs to their mothers. The sickly lamb they pushed into the centre of the flock, thinking that if the eagle came back it would find it difficult to separate the lamb from the others.

Soon all the sheep were fairly close together on the hillside, and Johnny counted them. They were all there except for the one poor lamb that had been stolen.

"Good dogs!" shouted Johnny to the two dogs. "Good Dandy! Good Shadow! You did that very quickly."

Both dogs wagged their tails. They always enjoyed their work, and would have done it even without orders from Johnny or the shepherd—but it was nice to have a word of praise. Johnny's father had told him that all creatures like a word of praise when they had done well, and should get it.

"Even little boys like to be praised sometimes!" the farmer had said with a smile.

The dogs lay down by Johnny. The boy was busy making a whistle out of an old elderberry twig. Andy had shown him how to do this, and he badly wanted one. At first he did not see that anything was wrong with the flock of sheep—but the dogs did!

They suddenly saw the sheep moving uneasily together and wondered why. Then they knew. In the sky was the great eagle again! The sheep, silly though they were, had a sense of danger, and were moving into a closer flock.

The dogs sprang to their feet with deep growls. Johnny dropped his whistle in alarm, for he had seldom heard such savage growls from the sheep-dogs. He saw the eagle at once.

It was soaring high as before, its great wings outspread, and the tips turning upwards. But every now and again the enormous bird looked downwards with its piercing eyes. It was looking for another sickly lamb!

"Get the sheep nearer!" ordered Johnny. The two dogs sped off. They raced round the flock, making them go nearer Johnny. One of the sheep escaped and jumped over a little mountain pool. Shadow went to get it back. He did not see that the sickly little lamb had been left behind a bush all by itself.

Johnny watched the eagle with one eye and with the other he quickly looked over the sheep. "Where's the other lamb?" he cried. "You haven't brought it in, Shadow."

The eagle saw the little lamb all by itself. It dropped suddenly from the sky like a stone, its claws ready to grip the life out of the little creature. But at the same moment Johnny saw the lamb too, and ran towards it. As he ran, he caught up a big stick belonging to the shepherd. He shouted and waved his arms as he went, and the dogs barked loudly and leapt around the boy.

The eagle checked its downward flight, and soared upwards again, still watching the lamb, which was now terribly frightened. Johnny shooed it towards the flock and it ran to its mother. The eagle watched it run. It had marked out that lamb for itself and its young ones. It could wait until the boy and the dogs were sitting quietly down again. Up into the sky it soared majestically.

Johnny could not stand and watch it all morning. He sat down again, but kept his eye on the big bird without ceasing. Then he noticed that two or three sheep and a lamb had wandered away from the flock again. He shouted to the dogs.

"Go and fetch them in, boys!" Off went the dogs like arrows. The sheep and lamb were silly and trotted off down the mountain-side as soon as they saw the dogs coming.

Just at that moment the eagle chose to strike again! Like a stone it fell from the sky, straight down to where the tiny lamb stood near its mother in the centre of the flock. It meant to bury its talons into the little creature and to carry it off before any sheep or dogs could stop it.

But Johnny was ready. He ran towards the dropping bird, shouting and waving his stick. The eagle now had the lamb in its claws, and all the sheep around scattered in terror. The lamb bleated pitifully.

"Drop that lamb, you cruel bird!" shouted Johnny, and he hit out at the savage eagle with his stick. But the bird was hungry, and would not give up the lamb. It was not such a cowardly bird as most eagles were, and it stood over the lamb, its wings half open, striking at Johnny with its curved beak.

Johnny hit at it again. The bird gave a strange yelp and rose into the air. In its feet it carried the lamb—but the little thing was heavy and the bird had to go to ground again to get a better grip. That was Johnny's chance.

He ran at it furiously with his stick, and the eagle had to let go the lamb to defend itself. It rose into the air just above Johnny and then swooped down on the fearless boy. Johnny knew that the eagle could hurt him seriously, but he did not think of being afraid. He lashed out with his stick.

The eagle swerved cleverly and came at Johnny again. The boy dodged—struck his foot against a stone, and fell heavily. He lay half stunned on the ground, and the eagle saw that the boy was at his mercy. He dropped like a stone on to Johnny, but before he could get his claws into the boy, Shadow dashed up.

He and Dandy had heard Johnny's shouts and had come tearing back up the mountain-side to help him. Dandy could not run so fast as Shadow, and it was brave Shadow who leapt on to Johnny's fallen body, and faced the surprised eagle.

Shadow growled so deeply and so fiercely that even the eagle was alarmed. The dog bared his great teeth and snarled. He would die for Johnny! The eagle could tear him to bits before he would desert his little master.

The bird struck at Shadow and tore a gash across his back. Shadow leapt up and snapped as the big bird struck. He got a mouthful of tail-feathers and the eagle yelped in anger. Its feet were feathered right to the toes, and its strong talons curved in readiness to strike again.

Johnny scrambled to his feet and picked up his stick. Then he saw something that gave him a shock. The second eagle was now soaring above him, waiting to drop down and help its mate. The boy was in despair. He could never tackle two eagles!

Then the flock of sheep took fright and began to run down the mountain-side. Down they went, helter-skelter, lambs and all. And Johnny could not stop them, because neither of the two dogs would leave him to go to round up the sheep! Dandy was now at his side too, and Shadow, of course, would not dream of leaving Johnny for the sake of the sheep.

The first eagle dropped down again, trying to strike at the boy's head—but with a magnificent leap Shadow jumped six feet into the air and snapped at the cruel legs. His strong teeth closed over them and he gave the bird such a bite that it yelped in pain and anger. Shadow's mouth was torn and bleeding, but the dog did not even notice it.

The bird was about to rise into the air again with a flap of its strong wings when Johnny took aim with his stick. He flung it with all his strength at the savage bird and hit it right on the back of the neck, where golden feathers gleamed in the sunlight.

The bird dropped down at once and lay stretched out on the turf, stunned. The dogs pounced on it and that was the end of the savage eagle.

Then Johnny picked up his stick ready to defend himself against the eagle's mate. But that bird was not so brave as the first, and when it saw what had happened it soared away and disappeared. Johnny flung back the wet hair from his forehead and blinked his eyes. He examined both dogs in silence and then bathed their wounds in the pool nearby. Neither dog was badly hurt.

"That *was* an adventure," said Johnny at last. "My word, I didn't like it at the time, and I'm glad it's over—but I wouldn't have missed it for worlds. Think, Shadow, we can go home with the eagle—we can show that we fought one, and that we won! We saved the other lamb. Oh, Shadow—oh, Dandy—whatever will everyone say?"

The dogs barked. They were longing to go down the mountain-side after the runaway sheep. They knew that it was their job to round them up again.

Down they went with Johnny. He carried the heavy eagle over his shoulder. The boy was proud and excited. He had not wanted to kill such a magnificent bird, but it was his duty to protect his father's flocks, and he had done so.

Andy, the shepherd, had met the sheep on his way up with the other three dogs and had got the whole flock together again. When he saw the dead eagle he was amazed.

"Do you mean to say that a boy like you won a fight with an eagle!" he cried. "Why, it's a thing that even a grown man might be proud of. You had no gun—only your hands and a stick. Well done, Johnny!"

"It was Shadow that really won the fight," said Johnny proudly. "He was so brave, Andy. You should have seen him!"

Then back to the farm they all went—sheep, shepherd, dogs, boy, and eagle. And what a time Johnny and Shadow had, telling everyone of their wonderful mountain adventure!

"It's fine to have a dog like Shadow," Johnny told everybody. And Shadow wagged his tail and barked loudly. "It's fine to have a master like Johnny!" was what *he* said, of course!